Matt grinned at Caitlin. 'How about a nice family outing one day while you're here? What about Sunday? I can make up a picnic lunch.'

Caitlin sniffed, blinking away the quick rush of moisture that blurred her vision.

The last thing she needed was a complication in the form of a man. Especially one with a child. Regardless of how charming they both were.

It wouldn't be fair to them... She didn't do relationships or family well.

She didn't know how to make them work, had no blueprint to guide her.

No, she had no business wishing she could see more of Matt and his precious son.

None whatsoever.

But the longing in her to be accepted, to be included, made it impossible for her to decline Matt's invitation. The way this family swept her into their centre delighted her and terrified her in equal measure.

Born in New Zealand, **Sharon Archer** now lives in County Victoria, Australia, with her husband Glenn, one lame horse and five pensionable hens. Always an avid reader, she discovered Mills & Boon® as a teenager, through Lucy Walker's fabulous Outback Australia stories. Now she lives in a gorgeous bush setting, and loves the native fauna that visits regularly... Well, maybe not the possum which coughs outside the bedroom window in the middle of the night.

The move to an acreage brought a keen interest in bushfire management (she runs the fireguard group in her area), as well as free time to dabble in woodwork, genealogy (her advice is...don't get her started!), horse-riding and motorcycling—as a pillion passenger or in charge of the handlebars.

Free time turned into words on paper! The dream to be a writer gathered momentum! And, with a background in a medical laboratory, what better line to write for than Mills & Boon® Medical™ Romance?

**This is Sharon's first book for
Mills & Boon® Medical™ Romance!**

SINGLE FATHER: WIFE AND MOTHER WANTED

BY
SHARON ARCHER

MILLS & BOON

Pure reading pleasure™

First published in Great Britain 2009
Harlequin Mills & Boon Limited,
Eton House, 18-24 Paradise Road, Richmond, Surrey TW9 1SR

© Sharon _____ 2009

ISBN: 9_____

Set in Times Roman 10/4 on 11/4 pt.
15-0509-51229

Printed and bound in Great Britain
by CPI Antony Rowe, Chippenham, Wiltshire

SINGLE FATHER:
WIFE AND
MOTHER WANTED

Thank you to Anna Campbell, Rachel Bailey and Marion Lennox—for your honesty when I asked for your opinion, and for fun, friendship and tons of encouragement.

Thanks, too, to my ever-patient medical friends, Judy Griffiths and paramedic Bruce.

To Rhonda Smith, friend and neighbour, who read this in an early draft and liked it!

To the members of Romance Writers of Australia for support, above and beyond.

And to Glenn: husband, hero and believer!

CHAPTER ONE

GHOSTLY gum trees loomed in the fog then slid away to the side as Matt Gardiner drove cautiously through the deserted countryside. With visibility reduced to metres, the route looked unfamiliar. No chance of using the craggy peaks of the Grampians as a point of orientation this morning.

Beside him sat his ten-year-old son, uncharacteristically quiet. Nicky Gardiner was in big, big trouble. Matt suppressed a shudder at the thought of the dangerous game Nicky and his friend had devised to entertain themselves. At this point, grounding for life sounded good.

Finally, Matt spotted the hazard-warning triangle he'd put out earlier at the site of Jim Neilson's accident. He pulled onto the verge behind a tiny sports car.

The vehicle's driver was crossing to the fence where Jim's truck and horse float had ploughed through into the paddock beyond.

As he unbuckled his seat belt, Matt watched a figure pick a path across the green swathe that the runaway truck had slashed through the frost. An elegance of movement suggested the person could be a woman. Bundled up in a huge padded black jacket and hat, she looked more like the Michelin Man.

Seven-thirty. He felt like he'd been on the road for hours. Between yesterday morning's delivery of a slightly premature baby and last night's acute asthma attack in one of his younger patients, he was beyond tired. With the respiratory emergency resolved, he'd been on his way home more than an hour ago only to discover the sometime horse breeder's latest debacle.

Nothing had been straightforward. Poor phone reception had meant a trip into town to organise the tow truck instead of a simple phone call. Which, as it had happened, had worked out well since he'd been close by to deal with the fallout from the boys' adventure. An overnight stay with a mate had ended with a sword fight with real machetes, for heaven's sake. He tamped down another shiver at what could have happened to the would-be elf lords.

Matt glanced at his son, stifling the fresh words of censure that threatened to bound off his tongue. Instead, he managed to keep it mild. 'Stay in the car, Nicky. I'll be back in a minute.'

'Sure, Dad.' At least he sounded subdued. Like he might have realised he'd pushed his father too far.

Frigid air seared Matt's lungs when he stepped out of the warmth of his car.

Steady, rattling thumps were battering the foggy tranquillity. From the confines of the horse float, Jim's four-legged passenger didn't sound happy.

Matt rubbed his face, enjoying the momentary relief of chilled fingertips against the lids of his tired eyes. He wanted to go home to bed, snatch maybe a half-hour nap before starting work. He shrugged away thoughts of quilt-covered comfort. No chance of that this morning. Not now.

He tucked his hands into his pockets and trudged after the driver of the sports car.

Brittle spears of frosty grass crunched beneath his feet and his breath plumed in front of his face. Winter was reaching into the second month of spring to give inland Victoria one final taste of its power. Hard to believe another two months could see them sweltering in the heat of the Australian summer.

He saw Jim scramble out of the cab of the truck. Frustration was obvious in every movement of his barrel-like body as he stomped back towards the horse float.

As soon as he let the man know the tow truck would be at least two hours, Matt could take his son home. Take time to have a serious talk. His heart clenched tight. Didn't Nicky realise how precious every single hair on his head was?

Even Nicky's mother, a very absentee and uninterested parent, would take a dim view of their son getting stabbed.

Ahead, the newcomer paused by the tangled wreckage of the fence. 'Would you need a hand, then?' a husky female voice called into a small pocket of silence.

Matt's stride faltered and his breath caught at the sound of the lilting Irish accent.

Ridiculous. He must be even more sleep deprived than he'd thought if a woman's voice could have that sort of effect.

Suddenly, all the tension of the morning coalesced and unreasonable anger flared deep in his gut. Why had she stopped at the accident? The truck and float were thoroughly bogged down. No way was her tiny sports car going to be any use. She was only going to get in the damned way.

From the paddock, Jim shot a disgruntled look in their direction before opening the trailer door to heave himself inside.

Matt drew level with the woman. 'Unless you can morph into the Incredible Hulk or you're a certified fairy godmother, there's probably not much you can do,' he said, not even trying to curb his sarcasm.

But as soon as he began to speak, she turned and fixed him with direct smoky-grey eyes. He swallowed. Brown curls peeped out from beneath the hat, curved onto her sculpted cheekbones and disappeared beneath her padded collar. She was lovely.

The package screamed affluence.

And sex appeal.

His pulse spiked.

'Is that so?' Even her voice was seductive. Deep with that intriguing foreign burr.

His gaze settled on her mouth. The full lips were lightly covered with a tempting gloss. Matt's mouth and throat felt parched.

He hadn't kissed a woman for a long time. A very, very long time.

Matt blinked as he struggled to direct his thoughts in a less unnerving direction. An apology. He was being obnoxious. She was a passer-by trying to do the right thing. He had no right to take his accumulated ill-humour out on her.

He twisted his mouth into a smile as he tried to dredge up the right words. The apology froze on his tongue as she tilted her head to look along the length of her perfect straight nose. Thick lashes swept down, narrowing her eyes to a dismissive glare. He felt as though someone had paralysed his rib muscles, trapping the air in his chest.

A frantic whinny and a shout from the stranded vehicle shattered the moment. The woman swivelled back to the trailer and his lungs resumed functioning.

He wanted her to look at him again. To speak again. 'Of course,' he said, as he walked beside her towards the horse float, 'a horse whisperer could be just as good as a fairy god-mother.'

'I might surprise you, now, mightn't I?' But she didn't bother to glance his way.

Jim shot through the door, backside first, as the float rocked under the impact of several solid thumps. It sounded as though the horse inside was trying to kick its way out.

After slamming the door, Jim turned to scowl at their approach.

'Problem?' said Matt.

'Uppity mare. Tried to take my arm off.'

Matt glanced down to see blood seeping between the man's fingers where he clutched his forearm.

He sighed. Home just got further away. 'You'd better let me have a look.'

The messy red fingers shook as they uncurled. Matt grimaced

when he saw the wound; large tooth marks scalloped the edges. 'Nasty. You'll need stitches.'

'It'll mend, I've had worse.' After a quick peek at his arm, Jim's florid cheeks turned an unhealthy grey. 'No need to fuss. I'm not one to see the quack unless I have to.'

'And a tetanus booster.' Matt was aware the woman followed as he escorted Jim to the flat tray of the truck. An occasional hint of her floral perfume tempted him to breathe deeply.

'Sit. Do you feel faint?'

'Of course not.' Colour washed back into the man's face.

'I need to get my bag.' Matt turned his head to look at the woman. 'If he feels faint, get him to lie down.'

'I don't need a nanny.' Jim set his jaw.

Silvery eyes slanted up to meet Matt's in a flash of unexpected communion. One brow arched expressively. 'I will.' Her lips twitched and he found his own curving in response.

He was left with the impression she'd be firm and efficient if Jim required her ministrations.

'What would be the problem with your mare, then?' the woman asked as Matt turned away. He heard Jim mumble a response.

As he made the return journey a few minutes later, having reassured Nicky that he wouldn't be long, Matt could see she still stood guard, arms folded. He gave in to temptation and ran an appreciative eye over her slender legs, feeling a sneaking regret that the warm jacket hid the rest of her.

She looked around at his approach and he found his pulse bumping all over again as the impact of her features hit him afresh.

He set his bag beside Jim, his fingers on the catch fumbling, oddly uncoordinated. How long since the proximity of a member of the opposite sex had affected him so badly? He couldn't remember.

'I didn't have the opportunity to play Florence Nightingale, more's the pity.' Her smoky eyes sparkled with humour.

'Better luck next time.' Good grief. It wasn't just his hands that fumbled at her nearness, it was his wits as well.

'Do you need a hand?' she murmured.

'What? Oh, no. Thanks.'

She stepped back. Half relieved, half disappointed, he snapped on a pair of latex gloves and turned his attention to the mangled forearm. After irrigating the area with saline, he probed the torn flesh, pleased to see no sign of foreign material in the wound.

He dried the surrounding skin after applying antiseptic then closed the ragged edges as tidily as he could with steri-strips. Digging around in his bag, he found a packet of sterile gauze dressing and a crêpe bandage.

The sounds from the float were quietening, he noted peripherally as he worked. At least that aspect of the problem seemed to be settling down.

With practised efficiency, he bound the gauze pad into place. It wasn't going to be pretty but at least it was cleaned and dressed. The chances of Jim coming into the surgery to have the thing seen to properly were minimal. He made a mental note to look up the man's immunisation status.

'If I haven't heard from you about the tetanus booster,' he said, as he taped the end of the bandage securely, 'I'll give Judy a buzz.'

'No need for that,' Jim said in a rush.

'No trouble.' Matt permitted himself a small smile as he stripped off the blood-smeared gloves. Jim's wife would make short work of any objections.

Bundling up the discarded gloves with the used gauze, he fastened the top of a small rubbish container.

Behind him, from the float, came a series of low gruff whickers and a few soft shuffling thuds. And the murmur of a soft feminine voice. He looked around.

Where was the woman? Surely she wouldn't…

He frowned at the curved perspex window of the trailer. It

was too scratched for him to see anything except the movement of blurred shapes. His gaze dropped to the black padded jacket draped over the drawbar. A sinking feeling chilled the pit of his stomach. 'Is she in the float?'

Without waiting for an answer, he set his teeth and spun towards the trailer. Did the woman have no sense? Now he'd have another patient for stitching...or worse.

Three long strides took him to the door. He was about to jerk it open when the significance of the soft noises from inside sank in. Forcing himself to calmness, he eased it back and looked inside. The smell of ammonia clogged his breath and he realised the floor was awash with urine.

Apparently unconcerned by the stench or the fact that her boots were getting wet, the woman was at the horse's shoulder, talking softly. The animal's long ears flicked in response to the soothing voice.

Without the bulky jacket enveloping her, the newcomer had a very nice figure. Matt froze, his feet rooted to the spot.

A *very* nice figure.

Naturally padded in all the right places.

The ribbing of her jumper accentuated a narrow waist and he could see the gentle curve of one breast.

Unaware of him, she bent, lifting the canvas rug, to look at the horse's belly. The way the black denim stretched across her rear had him drawing in a quick gulp of air.

'What's happening?' His voice sounded strained.

Two sets of eyes snapped around to look his way. The effect would have been comical except for the anxiety he could read on both faces.

'Could you open the back of the trailer, please? She's in labour.'

'She's in labour?' he repeated, his glance bouncing from the woman to the horse and back again. The words wouldn't form a reasonable picture in his head.

'You know...in labour? She's going to be a mother.'

'I know what in labour means. I'm a damned doctor.' He squashed a wave of dismay. So much for his hopes that the situation in the trailer had improved. 'I've just never had a patient with this many legs.'

'Isn't that a handy coincidence, then?' She arched a shapely, dark eyebrow at him. 'I'm a damned vet. Most of my patients have this many legs.'

And then she smiled. It was as though the sun had come out.

Matt blinked. She'd wanted him to do something…at least he remembered that much.

What was wrong with him?

CHAPTER TWO

DESPITE the seriousness of the situation, Caitlin Butler-Brown found herself smiling. As she watched the man absorbing this new crisis, the details of his face burned into her brain. Medium gold-brown hair, tussled as though he'd run careless fingers through the short thatch. Strong cheekbones and chin, stubbled jaw, slightly crooked nose. But it was his eyes that held her. An astonishing clear green and filled, right now, with naked disbelief.

With her hand on the mare's back, she felt as much as heard the shuddering groan, the restless shift to find a more comfortable position. Her concern switched instantly back to her patient.

'Perhaps you could hurry. She needs to move around, find a spot for her birthing.'

'Right.' He pulled back and the latch snicked softly behind him. Caitlin turned to soothe the fidgety mare.

'There, then, sweetheart. At least he's not the sort to blather on when a girl's got urgent business.' She kept up a steady flow of patter as she reached for the hitching rope and untied the knot. 'We'll have you out of here in no time.'

A loud clunk at the back of the trailer told her that the man was doing as she'd asked.

'Here!' At a shout from the cab of the truck, Caitlin glanced through the grubby haze of the window. A blob moved rapidly towards the trailer and then, down the side, out of sight. 'What're you doing?'

'Your master's not best pleased, darlin'.' She caressed the sweat-damp neck. 'Let's hope our intrepid doctor is up to the task of overruling him.'

Conditions were already less than ideal—without any obstructions from a belligerent owner. Caitlin tamped down the unease in her belly, knowing the mare needed her to be calm.

'Your mare's about to deliver, Jim.' The second bolt clattered back. Their rescuer wasn't allowing himself to be distracted. 'She needs to get out of the float.'

'But—' The protest was cut off as the ramp lowered with a grinding squawk.

Caitlin ducked under the chest bar and moved to the back of the float. When the doctor caught her eye, she sent him a grateful smile. His answering grin made her heart skip a beat and her fingers fumbled with the chain looped behind the mare's haunches.

She blew out a small breath. The man was far too distracting. Best to concentrate on her patient, she told herself sternly as she encouraged the mare to back slowly down the slope, step by uncertain step.

Mentally, she ran through the stages of a normal delivery. Heaven help them if there was a problem. She had her bag in the car, but any serious intervention could require more specialised equipment.

'She can't foal here.' Jim reached for the lead rope. The mare's ears flattened against her skull in clear warning and he snatched his hand back.

'It won't be perfect.' Caitlin decided to act as though his concern was for his horse's safety. Moving methodically, she unfastened the canvas rug and slid it off. She ran a professional eye over the heavily pregnant belly. The membranes of the placenta were just visible beneath the arched black tail. 'But don't worry. She'll manage, Mr…?'

'Neilson. You don't understand.' He waved his arms and the mare sidled away, rolling her eyes. 'I'm taking her to stud.

She's supposed to have her foal there so she can be put to Johnny Boy.'

'You've left it too late for that,' she said keeping a tight hold on her temper. 'She's in stage-one parturition.'

'What?'

Ignoring his confusion, she handed him the folded rug. 'Would you have a longer lead, Mr Neilson?'

His shoulders sagged. 'There's a lunging rein. In the truck.'

Caitlin bit back a retort when he stood clutching the canvas, staring uselessly.

'Get it for us, Jim.' The masculine voice commanded, reaching Jim where hers had not.

'Eh? Oh, right.' He set off towards the truck.

Caitlin shut her eyes briefly and puffed out a small sigh. 'Thank you.'

'No problem.' He gave her a lopsided smile, moving broad shoulders in a faint shrug. 'You looked like you could've taken a chunk out of his hide and I figure he's had enough free medical attention from me this morning.'

Her gaze was caught, trapped by the appeal of his smile. He had a lovely mouth, the sort to turn a girl's head if she was foolish enough to let it. Just as well she wasn't so daft as to be tempted by such superficial things. Her parents' relationship had taught her the danger in that.

And yet, mesmerised, she watched the curve slowly straighten. Now that it wasn't stretched into a smile, the bottom lip was plumper.

Kissable and—

The mouth pursed.

Oh, God. He'd caught her staring. Her heart stuttered as heat rushed into her face.

Flustered, Caitlin jerked her eyes away as long loops of rope were thrust into her hands. Relieved to have an excuse to move, she stepped forward quickly to clip the lunging rein to the halter.

This raw awareness of a man was so alien that she felt self-conscious and uncomfortable in her body. Even simple movements seemed stilted, graceless. She struggled to understand what was wrong with her. Where was the reserve that invariably scuttled her relationships? This was a fine time for it to desert her.

She couldn't be vulnerable now. She had a mission to accomplish. No time for sightseeing or holiday flings…or to be distracted by a gorgeous face.

Caitlin loitered by the mare for a moment then reluctantly stepped back towards the men, leaving the rein loose to give the animal as much space as possible. As though sensing her limited freedom on the long rope, the mare moved restlessly, her head down as she pawed at the ground.

After a few minutes, the expectant mother folded her knees and, with a drawn-out groan, lowered herself inelegantly. Strong contractions rippled across the huge brown stomach and the membrane bulge grew larger.

'Just give her a minute here, Mr Neilson,' Caitlin said, stopping Jim with a hand on his arm as he started to move forward.

'She needs pulling.'

'Perhaps, but we should give her labour a chance to progress naturally first.' Everything so far seemed normal but any ill-considered human interference could easily change that.

Caitlin's senses went on high alert as the younger man moved to stand closer. The action seemed almost protective and she felt at once steadied yet even more unsettled by his presence. Impossible.

'You're in luck this morning, Jim.' The deep, mellow rumble of his voice played havoc with her bouncing pulse. 'You've got the services of a doctor and a veterinarian on hand.'

Caitlin forced her lips into a reassuring smile. This was not the moment to reveal that her experience was in small-animal practice.

Jim stabbed a nicotine-stained finger in the direction of the horse. 'That's my prize standard-bred mare. If anything goes wrong, I'll sue.'

Caitlin watched him stomp off in the direction of the truck. 'Jim Neilson at his worst, I'm afraid.'

'Hmm. He's worried.' And perhaps not without good reason since the largest animal she'd treated in the last few years had been a lanky Great Dane.

'I feel like I should offer a blanket apology for Australian men. We're not all obnoxious, all the time.'

She swivelled her head to look up at him. 'Just some of you, some of the time?'

'Quite.' He grinned at her, his green eyes glowing with open approval. Her heart fluttered uncomfortably. 'You haven't met me at my best either, have you?'

She swallowed.

'Matt Gardiner. Local doctor.' He held out his hand. 'And you *are* the horse whisperer. Much more use than a fairy godmother.'

'No horse whisperer, I'm afraid. Just Caitlin Butler-Brown. Itinerant veterinarian.'

Glancing down as her hand slipped into his, she was very glad she'd already introduced herself. Long fingers closed around hers, causing a warm tingle that had her utterly focused on his touch. The sensation intensified when his thumb brushed over her knuckles.

'Even better. Glad to meet you, Caitlin Butler-Brown.'

She couldn't have replied if her life depended on it.

A grunt of pain from the mare gave her the will to reclaim her hand…and her mind. She curled her fingers into a tight fist to quell the lingering fizz of the connection.

She forced her mind to the job at hand. 'If I do need to scrub, is there anywhere handy I can get soap and water?'

'I have water in the car. And I've got a bottle of alcohol hand sanitiser in my bag.'

'That'll do the job. Thanks.'

The scratch and hiss of a match announced Jim's return. She realised he was beside her, puffing on a cigarette in agitated gasps. The smell of smoke hung, unpleasant, on the crisp morning air, but Caitlin couldn't bring herself to complain. She was glad he was there, a defence of sorts against the man at her other shoulder.

Long minutes crawled by as they watched the mare.

'Dad?'

Caitlin's system jolted. *Dad?* She turned slightly, aware of Matt doing the same, to see a slim boy of about ten standing behind them. Except for his dark hair he was the spitting image of the man beside her. Matt had a child. He was married...or at least very committed. A surprising disappointment stabbed her square in the chest.

'I thought I told you to wait in the car,' said Matt.

'But I wanted to see the horse.' The boy stared at the groaning mare.

'Mmm. That makes all the difference, of course.' He ruffled the boy's hair. 'Caitlin, this is my son, Nicky. Nicky, this is Dr Butler-Brown. She's a vet.'

'Nice to meet you, Nicky.' Despite her disturbing reactions about his father, she didn't have to fake a smile for the boy— he was adorable. 'You can call me Caitlin.'

'Hi.' Anxious green eyes lifted to meet hers. 'What's wrong with him? Is he sick?'

'No, not sick.' Caitlin glanced over at the mare and smiled again, knowing Nicky needed reassurance. 'It's a mare and she's going to have a foal.'

'Wow. A foal? Like...now?'

She chuckled softly. 'Yes, very much like now.'

'Can I watch?'

She looked at Matt.

He shrugged. 'Sure.'

'Thanks, Dad.'

Matt's eyebrows came together sternly. 'This doesn't mean you're off the hook, sport.'

'I know.' Nicky looked both angelic and cheeky as he grinned up at his father.

The loving affection in the look the two exchanged brought a lump to Caitlin's throat. Instinctively, she knew Nicky would never doubt his place in Matt's heart.

Her eyes stung as she turned away. It was like getting a glimpse into the way a family should work, one where love was given unconditionally. The kind of family she would never be a part of. The insight was stunning. Powerful. Beautiful.

The mare moved restlessly. Another contraction and the membranes ruptured with a watery rush. Caitlin's focus sharpened. Spindly legs and a tiny narrow head were clearly visible. The delivery should proceed quickly now.

The minutes stretched and her instincts began to clamour. She drew in a deep breath and held it for several seconds. Something was wrong.

She licked dry lips then turned to Matt. 'I'm going to need that alcohol sanitiser after all, please, Matt. I need to check the foal's position.'

'Right.'

Jim fidgeted, pulling at the waistband of his grubby jeans. 'What's happening?'

'Your mare's not progressing as quickly as I'd like now that her waters have broken,' said Caitlin calmly. 'Did you have any scans done on her through the pregnancy?'

'Nope. She didn't need 'em.'

So, no clues as to what the problem might be. Caitlin prayed it was a straightforward abnormal presentation. Anything more complex could be hard to deal with under these circumstances. And with Nicky there, too.

'Have you got any clean cloths in your truck, Mr Neilson?'

The cigarette dangling from the corner of his mouth bobbed as he thought about it. 'There's a bunch of towels the missus forgot to take out yesterday.'

They'd do. 'Could you get them for me, please?'

Jim nodded, casting the mare a worried look as he headed to his vehicle.

Matt was back with his bag and a bottle of clear gel.

She stripped off her ribbed jumper, looked for somewhere to put it. Matt was one step ahead of her. 'Grab Caitlin's top for her, please, Nicky.'

'Thank you.' She smiled at Nicky as he held out his hands.

He clutched the jumper. She could feel his eyes following her every move as she squeezed out a generous handful of gel and rubbed her arm from fingertips to shoulder.

'Are you going to take the foal out now?'

Without stopping her preparation, she sent him a gentle smile. 'I'm going to feel how he's lying inside his mother, Nicky. I think the wee fellow might not be in quite the right position and that's making it hard for him to be born.'

'Will it hurt?'

'The mare? It might make her a bit uncomfortable but we need to help her so she can push her baby out.'

'What can I do?' asked Matt softly, as she dosed one of his gauze pads with the alcohol solution.

'I'll get you to hold her tail away for me.' She knelt at the mare's straining haunches and Matt crouched beside her. Frosty dampness from the grass seeped through the denim of her jeans, chilling her skin as she waited for a contraction to pass.

With one hand braced on the mare's rump, she threaded her other hand beneath the spindly front legs as the foal's nose slipped back. She felt the knobbly knees, the bones of the mare's pelvis and then… the problem. Another pair of hooves. The hind legs were engaged. They needed to be manoeuvred back down the birth canal before the forequarters could slip free.

A long contraction gripped her arm in a punishing hot vice. Caitlin closed her eyes and breathed through the pain. As soon as the muscles released she pushed the tiny feet with all her strength. No movement.

Another contraction. She couldn't suppress a tiny gasp as the powerful muscles clamped around her flesh. She felt a hand on her shoulder, opened her eyes to find Matt looking straight at her.

'You're doing great,' he murmured. His green gaze drilled into her eyes, as though he could transfer his strength to her. Unexpectedly, she realised she did feel a lightening, an ebbing of tension.

She nodded once, felt the contraction ease. 'This time.' She pushed. The feet moved. A tiny bit at first, before slipping back under the foal's stomach.

'That should do it.' She slid her arm out and sat back on her heels. The ache in her muscles slowly subsided. Out of the corner of her eye, Caitlin saw Nicky's runners tiptoe to a halt beside Matt's knees.

The mare gathered herself for another huge push and the foal slid onto the ground. Steam rose from the ominously still little body.

'Is it okay?' whispered Nicky.

'Yes.' Caitlin knew the declaration was reckless. But she felt compelled to make it. And there was no way she was going to let the foal be anything else. Later she might be able to analyse her need to shield this child she'd only just met.

For now she had work to do.

A promise to keep.

CHAPTER THREE

CAITLIN leaned forward to strip remnants of birth sac from the foal's perfectly formed face and clear the small nostrils. She placed her hand on the chest just behind the sharp little elbow. The fine ribs felt impossibly fragile as she felt for a heartbeat. Relief surged as a pulse fluttered against her palm.

'Matt, can I get you to raise her hindquarters, like this?' She flipped a towel around the haunches and lifted.

'Sure.' He moved to take her place. Back at the foal's head, she blocked one of the delicate nostrils and blew a breath into the other, watching as the chest inflated.

Come on, little one. You can do it.

After the ribs lowered, a second breath. Her mind willed life into the filly.

A moment later, she was rewarded with a quiver of movement. A tiny snort.

Caitlin sat back on her heels and took a deep breath, hoping the others wouldn't see the tears that were perilously close to the surface.

'Let's move back and give them a little space,' she said, taking refuge in practical details. 'If the mare's comfortable she'll stay down for a little longer. The less intervention, the better she'll bond with her bairn.'

'That was awesome, Caitlin,' said Nicky shyly, as they

moved back a short distance. 'You gave it mouth to mouth just like we learned at swimming…only different.'

'Clever boy, Nicky.' She smiled at him. 'It is different. Horses can't breathe through their mouths like we can. So the filly needed mouth-to-nostril resuscitation.'

The foal sat up, the small head lifted unsteadily, looking comically lop-eared.

Now that the emergency was over, Caitlin began to notice the cold air on her bare arms.

'Here.' Matt held out his windcheater. 'Put this on before you get a chill.'

'Oh, no. Please, it's not necessary.' She turned away quickly to reach for the jumper Nicky was still holding. The thought of wearing something of Matt's was more than she could cope with. Too much like an embrace from the man himself, all that warmth and the delicious smell from his body would surround her. He was disturbing enough just standing beside her. 'Thanks, but this will do. It's only, um, an old top.'

Matt shrugged back into his windcheater. A sharp sting of rejection at her sudden withdrawal was uncomfortable.

'Look, Dad. She's trying to stand up.'

Sure enough, the foal's long legs scrambled at the ground. It seemed to be a signal to the mare as she heaved herself to her feet. She turned to lick the coat of her newborn, intently checking her baby over.

Matt smiled, his heart squeezing. In an oblique way the scene reminded him of Nicky's birth. The precious moment when his son had been placed in his arms, tiny hands waving as the infant had yelled his displeasure.

The mare became more insistent, with nudges to the miniature haunches. Spurred on by the encouragement, the foal manoeuvred awkward limbs, pushing up with her hindquarters until she stood, albeit unsteadily. She looked all leg and large bony joints. A few staggering steps took her to the mare's flank where she nuzzled determinedly until she latched onto the teat.

'Congratulations, Mr Neilson,' said Caitlin softly. 'You've a grand little filly.'

'With a little help,' said Matt, determined that Jim should give Caitlin her due.

Jim cleared his throat. 'I'd have managed.'

Matt opened his mouth but Caitlin was there before him with a sweet smile for the cranky old man. 'Of course you would have, Mr Neilson.'

Matt had the satisfaction of seeing the older man's double take.

'Ah. Yes. Well, anyway, er, thanks. Just as well to have a vet here.' Jim's mouth snapped shut as though he was surprised by the words he'd just said.

'My pleasure.'

Matt stifled an abrupt urge to laugh. She'd handled Jim beautifully, better than he would have, wringing reluctant gratitude from the man with nothing more than a smile.

'She'll expel the placenta over the next couple of hours now her bairn's nursing. You'll know to leave that well enough alone, of course.'

'Of course.' Jim shuffled.

Caitlin was obviously unconvinced because she went on smoothly with her warning. 'Any pulling could lead to infection or prolapse of your mare's uterus. If the placenta hasn't cleared in a few hours, you need to call your vet.'

Bloodstains marred the sleeves of her pink top. The knees of her jeans were dark with dampness and there was dirt on the toes of her boots. Matt had never seen a woman look more beautiful than she was right now. She was marvellous. That willingness to get in and get her hands dirty, literally, without worrying about her appearance. No complaints. A practical woman.

She hitched a shoulder to rub her cheek. Matt suddenly realised her hands were still wet and grubby.

'I've got soap and water in the car, if you'd like to clean up.'

She hesitated and for a moment he thought she was going

to refuse. 'I would, yes. Thank you. Goodbye, Mr Neilson. I wish you well with your mare and foal.'

'Yeah.' He cleared his throat. 'Like I said, ah, thanks.'

Matt walked silently back to the car listening to Nicky chatter to Caitlin about how he was going to tell his class about the birth. Now that the excitement was over, Matt had time to wonder more about her. Who was she and why was she here? If she was a tourist, perhaps he could convince her that Garrangay was a good place to use as a base for seeing Western Victoria. What were her plans?

Not that it was any of his business…but for some reason he wanted to know.

At the station wagon, he got out the water bottle and liquid soap.

'Did you want to wash…?' He indicated her arm.

'No. No, just my hands. Thanks. I can have a shower later.'

He tipped liquid into her cupped hands, watching while she lathered her slender fingers.

'Have you got far to travel?' He congratulated himself on striking just the right note of casual interest.

'I haven't, no.' She was going to be staying locally? Anticipation tightened his gut.

'What brings you out this way?' There was an odd suspended second when her movements seemed to falter. 'Holiday? Work?'

She'd resumed scrubbing vigorously and Matt wondered if he'd imagined the moment.

'Secret mission?' he joked, when she didn't answer.

Wide, startled eyes, dark with some suppressed emotion, flicked up to his and away. Was it guilt? Surely not.

'Could I have some more water, please?'

Silently, he rinsed away the suds and handed her a cloth.

'I'm between jobs,' she said, finally. 'I thought…. It seemed like a good opportunity to see something of Victoria.'

The answer was reasonable. But her reaction told him it wasn't the entire story.

'Are you staying locally? I can recommend somewhere that makes a good base for sightseeing.'

'Thank you, but…no. I—I have…plans.'

The change from competent, compassionate professional to tongue-tied uncertainty seemed odd. The frown pleating her forehead, the tight line of her mouth, the agitated way she dried her hands all screamed, *No trespassing*. Had he unwittingly touched on something personal…painful?

His gaze drifted over the rapidly clearing mist in the paddock as he mentally replayed the conversation. Nothing he'd said seemed unforgivably insensitive.

She was about to disappear from his life. Bemused by the compulsion, he nevertheless wanted to say something to tempt her to stay. But he'd already stumbled in a way he didn't understand. Regret tugged at him, leaving him off balance. Perhaps it was just as well she was moving on.

A kookaburra began to laugh, the great whooping chuckles echoing into the air. Abruptly, the sound stopped, leaving a profound silence in its wake.

He forced his mouth into a smile. 'If you're ever out this way again, look us up. We'd like that, wouldn't we, Nicky?'

'Yes!'

'You're very kind.' She smiled gently at his son.

By the time her grey eyes transferred their gaze up to his, there was no trace of warmth left. She handed him back the cloth. 'Perhaps you could invite your wife. We could make it a family outing.'

No puzzle about his misstep here. 'Ex.'

'Sorry?'

'Ex-wife. I'm divorced.'

'Oh. I'm sorry.' Pink spots flared in Caitlin's cheeks, her eyes shadowed with vexation. 'I didn't mean…'

'Don't be.' Matt said, wanting to make sure she understood. 'It's old history.'

Caitlin's mouth opened, then closed, her teeth biting her full bottom lip.

'Mum lives in Melbourne,' said Nicky, with a complete lack of awareness of the undercurrents in the conversation. 'She hardly ever visits.'

'I…see. Well, I—I should be going.' She looked towards the paddock. 'Please, be sure to tell Mr Neilson he shouldn't trailer the mare and foal for at least a week.'

'I'll tell him. It'll be a while before the tow truck gets here to pull him out. He'll have a chance to get used to the idea.'

There was a brief silence, then Caitlin held out her hand. 'It's been an interesting morning, Dr Matt Gardiner.'

'It has, Dr Caitlin Butler-Brown.' He squeezed her hand gently, reluctant to let her go. 'Drive safely.'

'I will, yes.' She retrieved her hand.

'Goodbye, then.' She smiled at Nicky. 'You were great over there at the foal's birth.'

'All I did was hold your jumper.'

'That, too, but mostly you were cool and calm when things weren't going so well. That's a big thing.'

'Thanks.' Matt watched as his son all but wriggled with pleasure.

Caitlin turned and walked to her car, aware of a lingering regret to be saying goodbye.

Her fingers were still warm from the pressure of Matt's hand. She'd been prepared for the zing of his touch this time. And it had helped. Just.

Father and son were watching as she slid into the driver's seat. She winced about her embarrassing mistake—though who could blame her for thinking there would be a wife and mother waiting for them at home? What woman in her right mind would let such a darling pair go?

But, then, her own mother had demonstrated time and again how much more important research was when weighed against a husband's or a daughter's welfare. Only the dogged persistence of Caitlin's father, following his wife around the globe, had kept the family together.

She started the car, put it in gear and accelerated away.

A glance in the rear-view mirror revealed Matt was still there, one hand on his car roof, his head tilted slightly. He'd gathered Nicky to his side with his free hand.

A shadowy shiver surprised her as she took a final glance in the mirror. Matt and Nicky's figures were now tiny. She shook her head, irritated by the illogical trend of her thoughts. The feeling that the man was important to her in some way was plain daft. As was her wayward delight that he was single. Single didn't mean available. He certainly wasn't available to her. No man was. Especially not a family man.

She turned the corner, almost relieved to be able to dispose of the last tiny physical trace of them.

Matt's presence lingered in her mind, though. A secret mission, he'd suggested. He'd been joking but the words had held enough truth to tip her off balance. She *was* here for a reason. Not underhand but not straightforward and open either.

How do you introduce yourself to an aunt who doesn't know you exist? How do you tell a woman that her long-lost brother died with an apology on his lips?

'Da, you've left me in an impossible situation.'

Caitlin sniffed, blinking away the quick rush of moisture that blurred her vision.

She was here to gather information, to decide how to handle this delicate family matter. There was going to be pain, that was unavoidable in the circumstances, but she wanted to minimise the suffering if she could...for herself, for her unknown aunt, for whoever else might be involved.

The last thing she needed was a complication in the form of a man. Especially one with a child. Regardless of how charming they both were.

It wouldn't be fair to them. She didn't do relationships or family well.

She didn't know how to make them work, had no blueprint to guide her. Her mother hadn't wanted children at all. While Caitlin knew her father had loved her, his first priority had always been his wife.

A grey cloud of gloom settled over her. Because now here she was in rural Victoria to see if she could reforge the ties her father had cut with his family decades ago.

And experience showed she'd inherited her parents' inability to make family relationships work.

No, she had no business wishing she could see more of Matt and his precious son. None whatsoever.

CHAPTER FOUR

STRUCK out big time. Matt's mood dipped as the MG rounded a curve and disappeared behind a stand of scrubby bush. Once upon a time, he might have managed a phone number.

Nicky shifted. Stifling a sigh, Matt roused himself.

'She's nice.' Nicky looked up. 'I like her.'

'Me, too, mate.' Perhaps just a tad too much. He couldn't put himself on the line in a relationship again, leave himself vulnerable the way he had with Sophie. That had nearly destroyed him. If he hadn't had to pull himself together for Nicky's sake, Matt wondered how he'd have ended up.

Since the end of his marriage his interest in female company had been precisely zero. A chance meeting with a little Irish veterinarian had changed that.

Maybe his foster-mother was right. Maybe he did need to get out more. She was always encouraging him to find a *good woman*. A partner for him, a mother for Nicky. Prospects were trawled under his nose from time to time. Doreen made no secret of wanting more grandchildren.

He'd have to put Caitlin Butler-Brown down to experience, as the one that got away, and make more of a commitment to his social life. The thought of leaping back into the dating game made him shudder. But leaping anywhere with a certain veterinarian for some reason seemed outrageously appealing.

Which showed that the scars from his marriage hadn't completely killed his masculinity after all.

One look and his wary heart wanted nothing more than to plop into Caitlin's clever, caring hands. He should be looking for a nice country girl. Much more sensible. Though perhaps not. He grimaced wryly. His ex-wife, Sophie, had been a home-grown Garrangay girl. And their marriage had been a total disaster.

'Let's go and talk to Mr Neilson and then we can head home.' With one last glance along the empty road, he followed Nicky back towards the float and truck.

Jim was watching the foal's increasingly confident forays.

'Your mare and foal need to stay here for at least a week. Vet's orders,' said Matt.

'A week! I can't leave her here that long,' Jim gasped.

'You don't have a choice,' Matt said. 'You were a damned fool to try and move her so close to foaling. And you know it. Caitlin hasn't saved your mare for you to risk the animal's life again. Organising agistment here until she's fit to travel is a small price to pay.'

Jim coughed and spluttered before he nodded grudgingly. 'Here, you'd better take this. Your friend left it.' He held out Caitlin's black padded jacket.

Matt's fingers sank into the down-filled softness and warmed instantly. Her perfume wafted up, the floral tang bringing a sharp memory of clear, smiling, grey eyes.

Resolutely, he tightened his grip. It was an expensive garment, the sort that someone would want back.

'Thanks. I'll get it back to her. Come on, Nicky.'

Whistling softly, he tucked the coat under his arm and set off across the paddock. He had a cast-iron excuse for tracking her down without looking like some sort of unbalanced weirdo.

He knew her name. Knew she was a veterinarian with delightful hints of an Irish accent. How hard could it be?

Nothing she'd said gave him a clue where she was staying, except that it was somewhere in the area. He knew where he'd start. With his foster-mother and her contacts in the local accommodation industry. If he had to, he'd work his way through every motel, bed and breakfast, hotel and hostel in the district.

The Grampians loomed over her aunt's bed and breakfast. Remnants of fog clinging around the base did nothing to soften the daunting majesty. Despite the late morning sun, Caitlin shivered. The stark, craggy range glowered down at her, challenging her right to be there.

Her stomach clenched as doubts suddenly swamped her. Perhaps she should have written first. Prepared her aunt. How would the poor woman react to having a stranger drop into her life without warning?

Not for the first time, she wondered if her father had had other siblings. Was there a whole host of aunts and uncles and cousins lurking in Garrangay? She swallowed as her heart skipped uncomfortably.

As it stood, she was the only child of parents estranged from any family they'd had. Martin Brown and Rowan Butler. Her family was a tiny unit, even smaller now that her father had passed away.

Three hundred kilometres away, in the comfortable suburbs of Melbourne, this whole venture had seemed simple. But here, on her aunt's doorstep, it seemed fraught with complexity. Her usual calm detachment deserted her completely, leaving her mouth dry, a sinking sensation in her stomach. The urge to get back in the car and drive away was almost overwhelming.

She shut her eyes. Waiting behind her closed lids was a clear vision of brooding, green eyes beneath a dark gold thatch of hair. Her eyes snapped open. *Dr Matt Gardiner.*

There was an intensity about him—and her reaction to him—that was unnerving. She'd read the interest in his eyes, seen it turn to curiosity after she'd fumbled with answering his questions.

Her cheeks warmed at the memory of her gauche behaviour. Stupid. He'd even provided a ready answer for her—a holiday. All she'd had to do was say *yes*. Instead, she'd hesitated and that stark tension had sprung up between them.

'We hardly ever bite our guests.'

She spun around. A pleasantly plump woman smiled at her from a few feet away.

Her aunt? Caitlin stared, searching the face, the friendly blue-grey eyes.

'Mrs Mills? I'm Caitlin Butler-Brown,' she said, pushing the words past the constriction in her throat.

The welcoming smile faltered, replaced by a peculiar, almost stunned look.

Oh, Lord. *Was it recognition?*

It *couldn't* be. Da had said his sister didn't know he'd even married, let alone that he'd had a child.

Her surname was Butler-Brown, no reason at all for Doreen to associate the hyphenated name with Martin Brown.

And, besides, everyone said she favoured her mother in looks. Except for her eye colour. The silvery grey came straight from Doreen's brother…Caitlin's father.

Suffocating panic made her want to retreat, snatch open the door of her car and drive away. Maybe she wasn't ready for this after all.

'I—I have a booking.'

'Oh. A booking. Yes. Of course you do.' The woman seemed to shake herself mentally. 'I'm sorry, dear. Come in. Come in. Let's go around the back. Did you want to bring your bag in now or…?'

'Er, I might leave it until later.' If her courage failed her, she could still make that dash for Melbourne.

'I thought you might have come a bit earlier. Oh, but I expect you've been sightseeing.'

'Mmm, yes. I have.' That was one way of describing her long morning. She'd found a public bathroom so she could have a wash and change her top. Then lingered over cups of coffee while she'd debated whether she'd continue with her plans or retreat back to Melbourne.

'You don't mind using the tradesmen's entrance, do you? I've been gardening. That's what I was doing when I saw you.'

Now that the woman had started, it seemed as though the sentences gushed out.

'I'm Doreen Mills.' She gave a small, embarrassed laugh and her hands fluttered briefly. 'But you know that. Call me Doreen, of course. We don't stand on ceremony. I've not long taken some muffins out of the oven. I got so involved with the broad beans I nearly burnt them. The muffins, that is, not the beans.'

'I…see.' Caitlin bit back an urge to giggle lest it explode into full-blown hysterical laughter. She waited for her aunt to lever off her dirty boots at the step.

'I'll show you your room. Then we can have a nice cup of tea.'

The house smelled of the muffins and lavender and lemon polish. Everything was spotless and tidy without seeming intimidating. It was…homey and welcoming. *Settled* in a way that her family's houses had never managed, Caitlin realised with a small sense of envy. It beckoned to her but at the same time left her feeling like an outsider, as though she could never quite belong there.

'I'll put the jug on, then.' The flow of words stopped abruptly.

'Doreen?' Caitlin frowned. Was her aunt looking a little pinched around the mouth? 'Are you all right?'

'Oh, dear, yes. Nothing to worry about. I'd better just…' Doreen rummaged in a large bag then pulled out a box and shook out a blister packet '…take a tablet.'

Caitlin glanced at the label. Glycerol trinitrate. Her stomach swooped on a quick flood of anxiety. Her aunt had a heart condition. 'You're having chest pain? How bad is it?'

'Mild angina, dear. I'll be right in a minute.' But Doreen

allowed herself to be led over to the table and pushed gently into a chair.

'Sit here now and we'll see how you're feeling.' Caitlin slipped into the chair beside her hostess. To her critical eye, Doreen's colour seemed good. Better now, in fact, than it had been outside. 'Do you want me to call your doctor?'

'No, no. Heavens no. Silly me. I've overdone it in the garden, that's all. I'll be good as gold after we've had that cuppa.' Doreen grimaced ruefully, her eyes glinting with affectionate humour. 'And Matt will just growl at me.'

'Matt? Your doctor? That wouldn't be Dr Matt Gardiner, would it?' An odd sense of inevitability settled over Caitlin.

'My son. Well, technically my foster-son, of course.'

'Of course,' said Caitlin faintly. That would teach her to ignore her earlier shiver of premonition. She wondered what else might be in store.

Doreen made a small grimace, looking resigned. 'I'll tell him tonight when he comes home.'

'Comes home?' Shock numbed Caitlin's tongue, making her stumble over the simple words.

'Yes. He's—' Doreen broke off, her head cocked to one side. 'Oh, dear. I'm not expecting anyone. I wonder if that's him.'

Caitlin had been vaguely aware of the sound of the crunch of car wheels on gravel. Now a door on the other side of the house banged shut.

'Him? You mean Matt?' Her voice wasn't much more than a squeak. She was still grappling with the idea that he *lived* here. It was too much to think that he might actually *be* here. *No.* She couldn't meet him again. *Not right now. Not without some time to prepare.*

'Yes. He has an uncanny knack of…. Oh, dear. Please don't say anything about my little episode, will you, Caitlin?' Doreen shot a guilty look towards the door. 'He's had such a dreadful morning, I don't want to add to his load today.'

'But—'

'Mum?' The rich, deep voice jolted Caitlin to the core.

She swallowed hard, clasping her hands together tightly in her lap to prevent her fingers betraying her internal shudders.

'We're in the kitchen.' Doreen gave Caitlin a conspiratorial smile.

'Something smells delicious.' Matt came through into the large kitchen-dining area. The easy smile on his face froze as his whole body seemed to do a double-take. Caitlin's brain played the scene in slow motion so that it seemed to progress inexorably from frame to frame.

'You.' He was obviously having trouble believing his eyes. 'You're here.'

'Yes,' she managed. She felt barely able to string thoughts together, let alone put them into words to form coherent sentences.

'Oh, you two have met.' Doreen sounded intrigued.

'Yes. At Jim's accident this morning. This is the Caitlin that Nicky was talking about. She delivered the foal.' Matt's disbelieving eyes stayed focussed on her face. Almost as though he expected her to disappear if he looked away.

'Oh, my. Nicky's going to be so excited to see you,' said Doreen.

Caitlin smiled weakly.

'So staying here was one of those plans you were talking about earlier,' said Matt.

'Yes,' she croaked.

'Then you'll be here when I get home later?'

She stared at him. Escape to Melbourne beckoned.

'Of course she will be, dear,' said Doreen. 'She's booked in for a week.'

'Bookings can be changed,' he murmured, his eyes all too knowing. 'Caitlin?'

She swallowed hard. 'Yes.'

His mouth moved into a small smile and a spark of humour lit the green eyes. 'Yes, you'll be here? Or, yes, bookings can be changed?'

'Um. Yes. I'll be here.' Why did she feel as though she'd committed herself to more than simple accommodation?

'Good.' He nodded with satisfaction. 'Right. I'll be off, then.'

'Do you have time for lunch, dear?' said Doreen.

'Had some, thanks. I just called in to pick up these files.' He shifted and for the first time Caitlin noticed he was carrying a wad of papers. 'I'll take some of whatever smells so good back to work with me, though.'

'Muffins. I'll get you something to put them in.' Doreen slipped away from the table.

Compelled to break the small ensuing silence, Caitlin asked, 'How—how did Mr Neilson take the news about not moving the mare and foal?'

'He accepted it. You must have charmed him.'

'As long as he doesn't rush it.'

'Here you are.' Doreen was back, holding out a bulging bag.

'Thanks, Mum.' He kissed her cheek then looked back at Caitlin. 'I'll see you later.'

She hoped the smile she gave him didn't look as feeble as it felt.

After he'd gone, Doreen sat down again. 'Thank you so much for being discreet, dear. I feel a bit mean, involving you like that. But fancy it being you who was there to help this morning. I should have put two and two together earlier—Caitlin is an unusual name. But when you introduced yourself…I was so…' She gave an embarrassed laugh. 'Well, I'm just a bit muddle-headed today.'

Caitlin bit down on her lip, wondering what her aunt had been going to say. 'Sure, and don't we all have those days.'

'Some of us more than others.' Doreen smiled, but her eyes were thoughtful. 'Have you always worked with horses?'

'Never. I'm a small-animal vet.' Caitlin raised her voice to speak over the whistling of the kettle. 'You stay here. I'll fix the tea.'

'Oh, but you're my guest,' Doreen protested as Caitlin crossed to the kitchen to where all the tea things were laid out.

'You've got it ready, all I'm doing is the kettle,' said Caitlin, as she reached for the switch. 'Matt's practice is in Garrangay, then, is it?'

'Yes, he took over from Bert Smythe when he retired. Matt's built the practice up, modernised it,' said Doreen proudly. 'Poor old Bert had let things go a bit in his last few years.'

Having poured the boiling water onto the tea-leaves in the pot, Caitlin placed everything onto a tray and carried it across to the table. 'It must be nice for you, having Matt and Nicky living here with you.'

'Yes, it is, though, strictly speaking, I live with them, of course,' said Doreen. 'Matt bought the place when my husband's health deteriorated and organised renovations to make things easier for us. After Peter passed away, I was rattling around, wondering what to do with myself. Matt suggested turning it into a bed and breakfast. Milk for you?'

'Yes, thank you.' Caitlin accepted the proffered cup. 'It's a grand old building.'

'My great-great-grandfather, William Elijah Brown, built it. He and my great-great-grandmother, Lily, were early pioneers in the district.' She gave a self-deprecating laugh. 'Don't get me started or I'll have you looking at all my old photos.'

A sharp quiver ran though Caitlin's stomach. The man who had built this magnificent place, who had worked and, with his wife, raised a family here, was her ancestor, too. Longing and sadness tempered a feeling of pride.

'I'd love to see them—the photos.' A sudden fierce need to put faces to the names pulled at her. And maybe it would lead in to a way to tell Doreen why she was here. 'I've always loved old photos, wondering about the people in them, what their lives were like.'

Doreen fixed her with a quick searching look, which changed

to a delighted smile. 'Well, it just so happens I love showing them off. Let's take our cuppa into the lounge, shall we?'

Caitlin's legs felt rubbery as she followed her aunt.

'I've put the best of the best in this album,' said Doreen, patting the sofa beside her. 'If you're really interested in what their lives were like, I've got a collection of newspaper articles I can show you some time.'

Doreen flipped through a parade of sepia-toned photos, pointing out an ancestor here and there with an amusing story. The formality of the poses, women in long dresses, men in suits and uniforms, held Caitlin enthralled. If she'd been on her own, she would have taken much longer to look at them.

'Is this you?' she said, when they came to a candid photo of a young girl with a woman and toddler taken outside Mill House. The gardens around the house were much simpler and the verandah looked as though it had been enclosed.

'Yes.'

'So that's...' Caitlin's throat closed over.

'Mum and my brother, Marty.'

Caitlin was ambushed by a paralysing breathlessness. The toddler was her father. *Her father.*

Doreen stroked the photo lightly with a fingertip, her face suddenly etched with grief. Moisture prickled Caitlin's eyes in sympathy and she had to look away.

Oh, God. How stupid to think that the photographs might have created an opportunity to talk about Martin Brown's death. Sorrow clogged her throat in a painful ball. No way could she speak about her father's death right now, even if she'd wanted to. Her own emotions were too raw, too close to the surface. She needed to be better prepared, to have the words ready, practised.

Doreen cleared her throat. 'Anyway, that's enough for today.' She closed the album with a snap. 'Finish your tea and then I'll show you your room so you can bring your bags in and get settled.'

'Oh. But…. Are you sure you're up to having a guest after your angina attack? I can easily arrange to stay somewhere else.' She pushed aside her promise to Matt about being at the house when he returned. After all, he hadn't known about the angina attack when he'd pinned her down about her booking. If Doreen needed to cancel, Caitlin wasn't going to feel bad about leaving.

'I wouldn't hear of it. Please. I'll be so disappointed if you leave now.'

'As long as you promise to say if it does get too much,' said Caitlin, after a small hesitation. Perhaps she could ask Matt if Doreen's health was strong enough. But that would involve breaking her aunt's confidence. Her life seemed to be filling with all manner of deceptions.

Doreen clasped her hands together in delight. 'Wonderful. And why don't you join us for dinner tonight? It's just a casserole,' she said quickly, when Caitlin would have refused. 'I've had it in the slow cooker since this morning so it's no trouble. None at all.'

'Thank you, that would be lovely,' Caitlin said, responding to the apparent underlying plea. Was it real or was she hearing what she wanted to hear? Letting her own yearning for family colour her judgement? After all, Doreen didn't know she'd just invited her niece to share a meal.

Doreen's face lit up with pleasure and an answering glow settled in Caitlin's heart. Matt would probably be there but this time she had the advantage of being able to prepare for their next meeting. She'd be able to handle him and this inconvenient attraction.

She had to…he was a part of her aunt's life.

Matt puffed out a breath as he stacked the papers on the back seat of his vehicle. He felt like he'd been punched in the gut.

Caitlin was here. In Mill House. *In his home.*

Not that she was here to see *him*. With his system starting to settle, he could recognise that she'd been as disturbed as he'd been by the coincidence. In fact, her reaction had been closer to horror.

He'd been so completely thrown that he hadn't thought of any of the questions that crowded into his mind now. Especially about her strange reaction to his comments when he'd helped her wash her hands earlier. He'd had the feeling that she was hiding something, but he couldn't imagine what.

He slid into the driver's seat, the wadded black lump on the passenger's seat catching his eye. Caitlin's jacket. He'd completely forgotten about it.

In the end, the chance to return the jacket had arrived with minimal effort on his part.

Always assuming, of course, that Caitlin was still here when he got home.

She'd said she would be.

He hoped she would be.

Mostly.

CHAPTER FIVE

MATT GARDINER.

Caitlin froze on the threshold of the lounge, her fingers tightening around the spine of her book until she was sure something would break. It'd been six hours since he'd walked into the kitchen. Six hours that she'd used to prepare for this meeting. She'd convinced herself she was ready.

But she was so wrong.

What was he doing in this room? Doreen said he and Nicky lived in an apartment upstairs. Shouldn't he have been tucked safely up there?

But, no, his long body was sprawled in a recliner, head tilted back on the cushioned rest, eyes closed. Dark shadows beneath his eyes made him look oddly vulnerable. The difficult twenty-four hours of routine work and after-hours emergencies that Doreen had described earlier must have caught up with him.

His mouth was slightly curved, the bottom lip invitingly full. Caitlin frowned. She didn't usually notice these details about men. To be sure, she didn't want to notice them about this man in particular.

A moment later, his mouth moved. Her eyes followed the tip of his tongue as it made a leisurely pass over his lips, leaving them glistening.

Stifling the need to gulp in air, Caitlin retreated, one painstaking step at a time. But the door, having opened so quietly inwards, gave a tiny protesting squeak at her attempt to shut it slowly. She stopped, her gaze snapping back to Matt.

The brilliant green eyes were open, watching her progress with interest. He smiled slowly, as he levered the recliner into an upright position.

'Well, well. Caitlin Butler-Brown. We meet again.' Straightening to his full height, he stretched briefly. The movement made the fabric of his polo shirt hug his leanly muscled torso. His well-worn jeans rode low on narrow hips. He ran a hand over his hair, smoothing wayward tufts. 'Come in.'

'I didn't mean to disturb you.' She clutched the book in front of her, a flimsy defence against his physical appeal.

'Bit late to worry about that, Caitlin,' he said cryptically, slipping his hands into the pockets of his jeans.

The gleam in his eyes made her feel like succulent prey venturing into a predator's lair. Instinct made her want to run, but she could find no plausible reason to refuse to enter the room. Especially since that had plainly been her intention before she'd seen him.

'Can I get you something to drink?'

'Not for me, no. Thank you.' The last thing she needed was alcohol. The unfamiliar pull of attraction she felt around him left her feeling skittish and vulnerable. Even the smallest level of intoxication might give her the illusion that she could handle him.

She sent him a cool smile and chose a chair beside the woodburning heater. Instead of returning to the recliner, he followed her across the room and sank onto the end of the sofa nearest her chair. The arrangement seemed uncomfortably intimate. In her peripheral vision, she could see his long legs stretched out, sock-clad feet pointing towards the flickering warmth of the fire.

'Mum tells me she had an angina attack while you were here this morning.'

'She did, yes.' Thank goodness Doreen had come clean, thought Caitlin. At least that was one deception off her conscience.

'Thank you.'

'For what? I didn't do anything.' Worse, she had a nagging concern that her arrival might have precipitated the attack. Though there was nothing concrete to confirm her suspicion. 'She had everything under control.'

'I know. But I like knowing someone was here with her.'

Caitlin hesitated a moment. 'Is she well enough to have guests? I'd rather not stay if you think it'll put her under too much stress.'

'She manages her condition pretty well.' He smiled wryly. 'Besides, I don't think I'd dare try to stop her running the bed and breakfast now. There's nothing she enjoys more than a houseful of guests to pamper.'

Guilt made Caitlin's smile feel strained. She wasn't *just* a guest, she was the bearer of bad tidings. Why had her father turned his back on his sister and this wonderful ancestral home for more than half a lifetime? He'd swapped the certainty of belonging for a nomadic life with her mother.

And yet, in the last days of his illness, it was this place and his sister that his thoughts had returned to—family that he'd left behind all those years ago. Would Doreen want to know the news that her younger brother was dead? Was she even well enough to handle it? No possibility now of reconciliation.

'So you staying here is a happy coincidence, isn't it?' Matt's voice rumbled into her musing.

'A happy coincidence?' she said blankly, trying to pick up the thread of the conversation. His comment, coming on the heels of her thoughts, jolted her badly. 'I—I'm sorry. What were you saying?'

Was he toying with her? Did he suspect there was more to her visit?

'I was wondering how I'd be able to track you down.'

'Why—why would you want to do that?'

There was a small, charged silence.

'I have something you'll want.' Laughter and something warmer lurked in his eyes as he leaned on the arm of the sofa and watched her.

Flirting. There was nothing sinister going on. He was just *flirting* with her, and her conscience had imbued his words with deeper overtones.

Just flirting? she mocked herself silently. A pulse thumped frantically in her throat and it was all she could do not to put a protective hand up to cover it.

'Is that so?' She swallowed, willing herself to relax. 'I can't imagine what it might be.'

'You can't imagine…anything?' His mouth tilted into a small teasing smile. 'I'm stricken.'

'Sure, and don't you look it,' she said, struggling to keep her expression bland.

'Perhaps if you tried harder, something might come to mind.'

'Matt, could you—?' Doreen's head appeared around the door. 'Oh, Caitlin. Sorry, dear, I didn't realise you were in here as well.' The older woman looked from one to the other and back again.

Did her aunt sense the tension in the room? Caitlin shivered. The interruption couldn't have come at a better time.

'Could you call Nicky in for dinner, please, Matt, dear? He's down by the creek.'

'Of course.' He got to his feet, sending a small smile Caitlin's way as he excused himself.

'That thing I have that you'll want.' At the door, he looked back at her. The small smile on his lips made her heart beat skitter. 'It's your jacket.' She looked at him blankly. 'From this morning. You left it on the towbar of Jim's float.'

'Oh. Yes. Thank you.'

She huffed out a sigh of relief as he left the room. She'd never felt this out of her depth with a man before. Was it just her private agenda making her so vulnerable...or was it the man himself?

'What are you hoping to do while you're here, Caitlin?'

Matt ladled casserole onto Nicky's plate before adding a scoop to his own.

'Oh, a bit of sightseeing. The usual tourist things. I've got a stack of brochures.' No sign of the hesitancy that had marked her answers this morning. Of course, she'd had time to prepare her answers. Or perhaps he was being overly suspicious because of his attraction to her...his instinct for self-preservation trying to find a flaw, a reason to reject the undeniable chemistry.

'You've come at a good time of year,' said Doreen. 'The wild flowers are out. And it's not too hot. It's a shame you're only here for such a short time. Maybe you'll come back again and visit for longer.'

Matt glanced at his mother. He'd never heard her use that wistful tone before with her guests. In fact, now that he thought about it, this was the first time a guest had been invited to the dinner table with the family on the very first night.

'Da-ad. I don't like broccoli.'

Matt was surprised to see a generous helping of the vegetable on the edge of his son's bowl.

'Oh, right.' After transferring the unwanted florets to his own plate, he reached for the beans and filled the newly vacant space.

Nicky wrinkled his nose in disgust but didn't protest.

'And after your holiday? You're back to work—in Melbourne, didn't you say?' He served some of the buttery beans for himself then glanced at Caitlin.

She looked serene, thick lashes hiding her grey eyes, cheeks lightly tinted with pink, as she broke open the roll on her side plate and reached for the butter. Why did he have the feeling that beneath the calm exterior she was weighing her answer, using the food as a delaying tactic?

'I'm between jobs.' She put down her knife and looked across at him.

'You've got something lined up?'

'Not yet.'

'What are you looking for?'

'Small-animal practice.'

'Carrots, Caitlin?' Doreen handed their guest the bowl.

'Thank you.' A tiny secretive smile crimped the ends of Caitlin's mouth as she took the dish.

'Not equine medicine, then?' Matt grinned at her as she switched her gaze back to him. He wanted to know more about her. It was sensible, he assured himself. If she was going to be spending time with his family, it was right to find out a few things. At least.

'Not equine medicine, no.'

'You've obviously had quite a bit of experience with horses, though.' Using his fork, Matt speared a chunk of meat. 'The way you handled the foal's resus this morning.'

'Dr Tonkin would be relieved to know he taught me something in his classes. That was my first solo as an equine midwife.' A mischievous gleam lit her eyes.

'In that case, Dr Tonkin can be proud of you,' he murmured, enjoying the irony of her confession. 'Just as well Jim Neilson didn't know.'

'It is.'

As the meal progressed Matt realised how thoroughly Caitlin charmed his small family. Nicky had already told him that he liked her. His son was beside himself with delight that she was staying here. And Doreen seemed very interested in her guest. Matt compressed his lips. *Interested* wasn't quite the right word. His mother's demeanour was closer to fascination.

'That was delicious, Doreen. Thank you,' said Caitlin.

'Oh, it was nothing special.' Doreen looked pleased and

flustered at the same time. To Matt's amazement a faint blush tinted his foster-mother's cheeks.

'That's where you'd be wrong,' said Caitlin. Matt shifted his gaze, catching the soft, unguarded expression on their visitor's face. The admiration between the two women was obviously mutual. But there was something else about Caitlin's look that made him curious…. What was it exactly? Hope? Longing? And maybe a touch of sadness. 'I've survived on my own cooking. Now, *that's* nothing special.'

'Well, thank you, dear.'

'Are you going to be here on Saturday, Caitlin?' Nicky's question diverted everyone's attention.

'I am, yes.'

'Maybe you can come to the show.'

'The show?'

'The Garrangay A and P Show. Agriculture and produce,' Matt added at Caitlin's blank look.

'What a wonderful idea,' said Doreen enthusiastically. 'Matt will be on duty, of course, but you can come with us. Can't she, Nicky?'

'Yeah. An' maybe you can watch me ride Sheba. If you want to. 'Course, you'll probably be busy.' The ultra-casual attitude didn't mask the underlying need in Nicky's voice. Matt tightened his lips, stopping the words of caution that lay on his tongue. His son's willingness to invite rejection, to take chances and stay open with people amazed him. And…shamed him, he realised. He toyed with his wineglass, waiting for her answer as acutely as Nicky.

'Now, that sounds really grand.' The smile she gave his son made Matt lift his glass and take a gulp of wine.

'And I'll be putting my jams in again this year,' said Doreen. 'As well as my roses.'

'There's usually not too much for me to do,' said Matt, beginning to feel cut out of the arrangements. Was that petulance he felt? How juvenile…and more than a little disturbing.

'Overdoses on fairy floss or the Ferris wheel, ice for bruises after the three-legged race, the odd stitch or two after the sponge-cake judging.'

From the glow of humour in Caitlin's eyes, he was sure she'd detected the faint peevishness in his voice. He wasn't at all sure he liked being so easy to read.

'Matthew! That's only happened once.' Doreen gave him a brief reproachful look. 'Agnes was so excited about winning the sponge section last year that she tripped on the leg of a trestle table.'

'Perfectly understandable.' Caitlin's mobile mouth twitched.

'Well, it was her first win. Anyway, I'm sure you'll enjoy the day, dear,' said Doreen. Oblivious to the undercurrents, she picked up the leftover casserole and went through to the kitchen.

Caitlin rose and gathered up the dirty plates. Matt let his gaze follow her across to the sink. Their guest was a pleasure to watch, moving with a natural fluid grace. Casual dark grey trousers clung to gentle curves and her tailored red shirt nipped in at the waist. The overall look was sex appeal without flaunting it.

On the other hand, he'd probably have found her close to irresistible in anything. Hadn't he been attracted this morning when she'd been up to her elbows in horse blood and after-birth?

Caitlin stopped beside his mother, who laughed at something she said.

He frowned as he watched them.

Caitlin Butler-Brown was a walking, talking, red-blooded woman, intelligent, good looking, the right age. All the attributes that would normally have had his mother's worst match-making instincts on high alert.

What was going on here?

Last year, she tried to fix him up with a date on show weekend and he'd been working then, too.

Perhaps it was because Caitlin was a guest. Or was his mother trying a bit of reverse psychology? He could tell her it wasn't necessary. He was already interested in Caitlin Butler-Brown. Though, if she was only here for a week, they could have nothing more than a flirtation. Perfect, because he'd been out of the dating scene for so long, he wasn't ready for anything more.

So, a nice, short flirtation. For a week, he'd enjoy her company. No strings attached.

'And you must see the Grampians while you're here, Caitlin.' Doreen came back towards the table, using oven mitts to carry a pie from the oven. As soon as she'd put the hot dish on the trivet, she pinned Matt with a brief, meaningful look. 'How about a nice family outing one day while you're here? What about Sunday, Matt? I can make up a picnic lunch.'

Ah, there it was, the unquenchable matchmaking spirit that he knew so well. Matt smothered a laugh. His foster-mother thought she was being subtle, bless her.

He cleared his throat. 'Sure, Sunday sounds good.'

'Oh, but you don't have to include me in your family plans.'

'We want to, Caitlin.' Another significant look from Doreen to Matt as she handed him a wedge of apple pie. 'Don't we, Matt?'

'Yes, that's right.' He grinned at their guest and earned a stern look from stormy grey eyes in return. His pulse surged. 'We want to, Caitlin.'

'It'll be so much nicer for you to go with someone who knows their way around. Won't it, Matt?'

Caitlin subsided into her chair with an odd helpless expression on her face.

'So much nicer.' Matt lifted a spoonful of dessert and met Caitlin's eyes over the mound of steaming fruit. It was perversely enjoyable to see someone else fidget under Doreen's well-meant manipulations. He might regret falling into line down the track when he tried to resist his mother's next match-making target. But for now he wasn't looking any further ahead than Sunday. 'Just say yes, Caitlin. It'll be so much easier.'

'Well, if you're sure…'

'We're sure.' He assured himself that he wasn't about to make the mistake of getting involved with someone who belonged in Melbourne. This was just a day out while Caitlin was here. It would be fun. And maybe he could indulge in that flirtation he'd been contemplating.

A bit of practice.

Keep it light.

Don't get in deep.

No one would get hurt.

'Hurry up, Dad! Caitlin!' Nicky called over his shoulder. 'Did you know possums only come out at night, Caitlin?'

'Yes, I did.'

Dusk was crisp with the promise of an overnight frost as Caitlin trailed Nicky across the yard. A wash of delicate pastels coloured the sky, leaving a lovely peach on the western horizon where the sun had just dropped below the Grampians.

Matt walked beside her. Out of the corner of her eye, she could see the torch swinging from his hand. She was glad of his silence while she turned over her thoughts.

She jammed her hands deeper into her jacket pockets. What was she doing here?

The short, simple answer was that Doreen had refused help with the dishes and Nicky had insisted that she should see the ringtail possum that he'd found earlier.

The longer answer was more difficult. The longing in her to be accepted, to be included, had made it impossible for her to decline Nicky's invitation. The way this family had swept her into their centre delighted her and terrified her in equal measure.

Dinner had been a revelation. Was it like that every meal they shared? Everyone's contribution was valid, encouraged.

Enjoyed. Including Nicky's. Nothing suggested that the warmth had been staged for her benefit.

The contrast to her family couldn't be more pronounced. Her mother's intense technical discussions with her fellow researchers had left Caitlin feeling isolated and lonely at the table.

She wondered if she felt it acutely with this particular family because she was related to Doreen. And because of her reaction to Matt.

'Penny for them.'

'Oh, I—I couldn't take your money.' She smiled to take the sting out of her refusal. 'You'd feel short-changed.'

She was glad when a few steps more brought them to where they were waiting to point out their find.

'Shine the light up there, Dad.'

Matt halted in the doorway and played the beam as directed.

'Come and look, Caitlin. She's still here.' Nicky grinned at her.

Matt turned his head, meeting her eyes. The small smile playing around his lips told her that he guessed exactly why she was hanging back. To see, she would have to move close, to stand at his side. Her heart hammered so hard she wondered what the statistics were on myocardial infarcts in twenty-nine-year-old females.

She swallowed and stepped forward, keeping her eyes on the finger of weak torchlight. A slim white tail hung down from a wooden beam and, after a moment, a pair of round eyes and a pink nose appeared on the other side of the upright.

'Oh, she's gorgeous.'

'Yes, she is.' Matt's soft murmur in her ear jolted all the way to her soul.

'Dad says they can have lots of nests. We found this one last week but this is the first time she's been in it when we've looked.'

'Well, thank you so much for showing me.' Caitlin moved

back. She needed to escape. Get away from the man standing beside her. Give her system time to recalibrate. 'I'll leave you to watch her. I'm going to…um, see if there's anything I can do for Doreen.'

She took care to make sure her gaze skimmed quickly over the pair, not letting Matt's eyes snare hers. If he thought she was running away…too bad.

CHAPTER SIX

MATT looked through the theatre-viewing window. The gloved and gowned local veterinarian worked on a cloth-draped hump. Bob Fryer's nurse, Haley, stood at the head of the table, monitoring the anaesthetic and checking her watch.

She glanced up, lifting a hand, and must have said something because her boss glanced at Matt over the top of his mask. Matt pointed to the door and Bob nodded briefly before turning back to his patient.

The pulse monitor's regular beeping was audible as soon as Matt pushed open the door. After tying a mask over his nose and mouth, he moved forward to look over Bob's shoulder.

'I can…feel…. Ah, that's got it.' Bob pulled a small mass from the cavity and dropped it into a kidney dish with a dull clunk.

There was something vaguely familiar about the object but, because of a coating of greenish slime, Matt took a moment to identify the foreign body as a shapely torso.

'A Barbie-ectomy.'

Bob chuckled his appreciation. 'This dog's got eclectic eating habits. Last time, it was a piece of plastic currycomb. It's a shame I can't put in a zip instead of sutures.'

Belying the grumbling words, the vet quickly closed the opening with a neat line of stitches.

'Okay, Haley, let's bring him round.' Bob peeled off his

gloves, pulled off his mask and slanted a resigned look at Matt. 'What brings you out this way? Thinking of changing the shape of your patients?'

The comment zapped Caitlin back into Matt's thoughts. He'd managed to banish her from his mind for the day...well, most of the day.

'I was just passing.'

'Just passing.' Bob snorted his disbelief as he dropped the used gloves into a bin. 'Yeah. Right.'

Matt watched as the stocky veterinarian walked over to the cupboards at the end of the room and rummaged through the contents.

'You cancelled your appointment today.'

'Too busy.' A moment later Bob re-emerged, a large clear plastic arc in his hand. Back at the table, he clipped it around the dog's neck to form a wide collar.

'If you'll get the door, Haley, I'll carry him through. Back in a minute, Matt.' He lifted the groggy Labrador off the table. 'I'll just get young Rex here settled.'

'I'm not going anywhere.'

'I was afraid of that. Wait in my office if you like,' he said as he manoeuvred through the door. 'We might as well be comfortable while you read me the Riot Act.'

Matt wandered through to the office, collecting his medical bag as he went. The room doubled as a tearoom so there were several armchairs, cosy if a little threadbare, grouped around a coffee-table in one corner. Putting his bag on the desk, he relaxed into the swivel chair.

Posters of the life cycles of various parasites were pinned around the walls. Egg to larva to adult, all depicted in vivid colour. Worms in dogs and cats and horses.

His gaze stopped at an unpleasantly graphic photograph of a dog's heart. The organ had been sliced open to reveal a tangle of thin white worms. This was the sort of thing Caitlin would encounter in her job.

Matt grinned. How would she react to knowing that a bad case of heartworm had turned his thoughts to her? Would she find it amusing? He rather thought she might. She seemed to have a quirky sense of humour.

Very different to his ex-wife. Sophie was serious. Always. She'd never had time for the light-heartedness that he'd tried to bring to their marriage. He suddenly realised how stifling that had been. Very commendably committed to her studies, then to her research and career...but not to their relationship.

He didn't want to think about that now.

Instead, he leaned back in the chair and looked up at the heartworm poster. What was Doreen's Irish guest doing today?

When he and Nicky had trooped downstairs to make their farewells that morning, she'd been in the kitchen having breakfast. Fresh-faced and impossibly young looking with that tumble of ringlets curling from a ponytail onto her shoulders. What would she have done if he'd given in to the impulse to kiss her goodbye? Not a peck on the cheek, as he'd done to his foster-mother. Oh, no. He'd tug off her fancy hair clip and plunge his fingers through those luxurious curls to tilt her face up. And then he'd press his lips to hers. Caress her, taste her.

Test her.

Straightening abruptly, he opened his eyes. Test *himself* was closer to the mark. If he didn't stop his mind straying off into these little fantasies, he'd be a basket case. At thirty-four, he was too old to be suffering an adolescent crush. But a bad case of the hots...now, that was something else again.

'Haven't you got better things to do than chase me around?' Bob's gruff voice jolted Matt back to the present.

'Business is slow.' Swivelling the chair to face his belligerent patient, he grinned unsympathetically. 'I'm having to run my more uncooperative patients to ground.'

'Must be.' Bob sank tiredly into the second office chair. 'I heard you dredged up a bit of my business the other morning.'

'I had help.'

'I heard that, too. To quote Jim Neilson, "a slip of a girl".' He chuckled. 'And all of about twelve years old if he's to be believed.'

'Caitlin's a bit older than that and a damned competent vet. Jim was bloody lucky she came along when she did.' Matt winced inwardly at the raw conviction in his voice.

'Jim did mumble something along those lines, too.'

In an abortive attempt to deflect the speculation he could see in Bob's eyes, Matt said the first thing that came into his head. 'She's staying at Mill House.'

'Is she indeed?'

Before he could dig himself any further into the hole he'd made, he snapped open his bag and removed the long metal case of the sphygmomanometer.

With a sigh of resignation, Bob rolled up his sleeve.

'Taking your medication?' Feeling more in control, Matt wrapped the inflatable cuff around the bare arm.

'Forgot this morning. Took it at lunchtime.'

'Checking your blood sugar regularly?' Matt hooked in the earpieces of the stethoscope. After locating the steady pulse beat, he pumped up the cuff and placed the diaphragm onto Bob's arm.

'I've been busy.'

'Uh-huh. So, have you been checking your blood sugar?'

The mercury dropped until the sound of the surging pulse started again and then a moment later stopped. Taking note of the reading, Matt released the air.

Bob swore softly. 'Sometimes.'

'How's it been?'

'Up and down.'

'You eating properly?' Matt looped the stethoscope around his neck and unwound the cuff.

'What are you? My mother?'

'No. Should I get her involved?'

'You wouldn't!'

Matt slipped his instruments back into his bag and sat down. There was a small silence while he examined his friend's face, noting the dull, tired eyes, the unhealthy greyish cast to the man's skin.

'How's Gary?' he asked softly.

'No change.' Bob's voice was rough with emotion.

Matt's heart went out to him. He knew that the bone-marrow transplant Bob was pinning his hopes on for his gravely ill son had had to be delayed because the donor had had an upper respiratory tract infection.

'Any chance of getting some relief so you can go down and be with Sally again?'

Bob snorted in disgust. 'Had a locum all fixed up but the silly bloke broke his leg. Compound fracture of the femur. Horse riding, of all things.'

'How about someone from Hamilton?' Matt rubbed his jaw as his thoughts raced ahead. *How about Caitlin?* She'd said she was looking for a small-animal practice. How would she feel about somewhere that covered large animals as well? The pregnant mare had presented no problems for her the other day.

'Someone's covering for a couple of days after the show.'

'They can't cover longer?'

Caitlin had only planned to be here for a week. Would she be prepared to stay longer to help out? His primary concern was for his patient, of course, but if she stayed he'd have a chance to get to know her better. Was that a good idea or not? He might want more than a flirtation. He might start to think about getting involved.

Getting to know her could be…complicated. She was a city person. Like Sophie had become. And look where that relationship had ended up. In the ditch. They'd fought over everything until Sophie's final betrayal.

'They're having their own staffing hassles at the moment with that gastric virus that's going around.' Bob grunted. 'So give me the bad news.'

'Your blood pressure is one sixty-four over eighty-six. Not good for a diabetic. Sounds as though your blood sugar isn't under control at the moment either.' Matt leaned back in the chair as he contemplated his patient. 'Do I need to paint the picture here?'

'No.'

'You'd be happy to have a locum if you could get one?'

'You're thinking of your little Irish lass?'

Bob's phrase made Matt want to wince. 'I'm thinking of Caitlin. Yes.'

'The thought crossed my mind when you mentioned she was staying at Mill House. You think she'd be interested?'

Would she? Did he want her to be? 'I'm...not sure.'

'No harm in asking, though, is there?' Bob grinned, looking suddenly more cheerful.

'None at all.' Matt put his personal doubts aside. Bob needed relief. 'Why don't you drop around tonight? Come for dinner. Mum'll enjoy an opportunity to feed you.'

'I'll be there.' He rubbed his hands together. 'I'm looking forward to meeting your Caitlin.'

Matt bit down on the urge to correct the impression that Caitlin was his. He had the uncomfortable feeling he'd revealed far too much already. Reaching into his bag, he plucked out a screw-top specimen jar and handed it to Bob. 'We might as well see what you're doing to your kidneys while I'm here.'

Standing alone in the room, Matt felt a chill pass over him. What had he done? Caitlin had been at Mill House for three days now. If she unsettled him this much in such a short time, what would the *little Irish lass* do to him after several weeks?

CHAPTER SEVEN

LAUGHTER carried down the hall from the study. Matt's lips curved. Homework? Enjoyable? That was a first.

Doreen said Caitlin had volunteered to help Nicky with a project on marine biology after accounting herself as something of an authority on the subject. An unusual string to the bow of a small-animal veterinarian surely.

The thought highlighted the fact that she was a stranger. A stranger he was about to invite to spend even more time in their lives.

He slowed as he neared the room, listening to Nicky's giggles and the lower-register chuckles from Caitlin.

The door to the study was ajar. He pushed it gently and absorbed the sight of the studious pair sitting at the desk. Caitlin's head was tilted towards Nicky's as they both focussed on the computer screen. Seeing them together gave Matt an almost uncomfortable feeling—part warm, part protective. The time she gave freely to his son got under his guard, disturbed him. As did Nicky's obvious response. He blossomed under Caitlin's attention.

Perhaps Doreen was right, perhaps he should be looking for someone. A wife and mother to complete their family unit. Unfortunately, it had been hard to want to cast anyone in the role.

Until Caitlin's arrival.

But what did he know about her apart from the fact that she was a veterinarian? And a city girl in Garrangay on holiday?

A city girl. Like his ex-wife. Though he knew it wasn't fair to measure Caitlin against Sophie's behaviour. Her infidelity had had nothing to do with location and everything to do with her lack of commitment to their marriage…to him.

He folded his arms and leaned against the doorjamb, trying to analyse the direction of his thoughts. Caitlin as flirtation practice for his rusty skills was one thing…sizing her up as mother material for Nicky was something else again. The idea had disaster written all over it.

And if she stayed longer, his son was going to get more attached to her.

He dragged a hand down his face. The idea of Caitlin working and living in Garrangay seemed suddenly, subtly threatening.

She leaned forward to point to an icon and murmured something to Nicky. Seconds later, a full-screen picture of a walrus appeared.

'Cool!' Nicky said, nearly bouncing with enthusiasm.

Matt watched a moment longer then, shaking off his forebodings, he said, 'I must be in the wrong house. This sounds like way too much fun to be Nicholas Gardiner doing his homework.'

Although his eyes were on Nicky, Matt still noticed a stiffening of Caitlin's posture. Intriguing. So, that feeling of reserve he got from her wasn't just his imagination.

'Dad!' Nicky swivelled on the chair and beamed at him. 'Caitlin's helping with my project.'

'So I heard.' He met Caitlin's gaze. The lovely grey eyes were guarded. No sign of the laughter she'd shared with Nicky only moments before. As he watched, a rosy glow tinted her cheeks. His heart bumped hard.

'Will you look at that? Time got away from us. Did you need the study?' She looked away, her hands fluttering over the pages of the book on her lap. 'We've nearly finished.'

'No need to hurry on my account,' he said, straightening up

and sauntering into the room. He propped himself on one corner of the desk. Her reaction surprised him, pointing to a vulnerability he hadn't seen since her first day here.

'See all these pictures, Dad. I'm going to use them to make my poster. We found heaps of stuff about marine mammals.'

'Great.' Matt looked at the papers, his heightened senses attuned to Caitlin's every move. He realised that the book on her lap was a black leather organizer, which she was now shutting.

Nicky grabbed a piece of paper off the printer. 'That's the last one, Caitlin.'

'So it is.' She succeeded in dragging the zip closed on the bulging pages. 'We need to find you some scissors and glue.' The smile she aimed at Matt was tight as she rose from the chair. 'There, now. The study's all yours.'

'Before you go, Caitlin, there is something I wanted to talk to you about.' Matt stood, feeling oddly as though he loomed over her.

She eyed him warily. The hand she rested on the back of the chair clenched, the knuckles pale.

'How about asking Nanna to get the scissors for you, Nicky? Caitlin and I won't be long.'

'Sure, Dad. See you in a minute, Caitlin.' Nicky flashed a quick happy grin at her before racing out of the room.

Matt crossed to the door and pushed it shut. The move created an unintended intimacy. Should he reopen it? Frustrated with his indecision, he left it closed and stalked back towards the desk.

'This looks dire. Should I be standing on the mat, then?' The lightness in Caitlin's voice sounded forced.

'What? Oh, no. It's nothing too serious.' He tried for a reassuring smile but it felt stiff and unnatural. 'Grab a seat.'

She slid back onto the edge of the chair, her movements not as graceful as usual. The black case was clutched to her chest as though it might protect her in some way.

He suppressed a sigh. A witty quip might diffuse the tension but he couldn't think of anything with his mind clogged with acute awareness of her.

And now that he had her attention he wasn't sure how to begin. Perhaps she wouldn't appreciate him having semi-volunteered her services.

He pulled out the other chair and sat. The silence lengthened as he contemplated her knees, held primly together, so close to his. After a moment, she laid the organiser across her thighs and, abashed, he wrenched his gaze up to meet hers. She looked confused, anxious. And no wonder. He'd shut himself in with her and now he was ogling her legs.

'Caitlin—'

'I apologise, Matt.' She'd obviously decided to tackle him head on but he wasn't sure where she was heading.

'Pardon?'

'I should have asked you before I helped Nicky with his homework. Doreen didn't object when I offered so I thought… But you'd rather I didn't, then?'

'No. No, it's not that. I mean, I'm happy for you to help. But it's not much of a way for you to spend your holiday.' He was making a hash of this. 'Though, actually, that's what I wanted to talk to you about.'

'My holiday?'

'In a roundabout way. Do you like Garrangay?'

A frown pleated her forehead. 'Sure. What's not to like?'

'How would you feel about staying longer?'

'Longer?' She stared at him blankly. 'Well, it'd be grand but I can't afford to.'

'But if there was a job, a locum position?'

'A locum?' said Caitlin slowly.

'For the local vet.'

'I see.' Her eyelashes swept down, hiding her expression. Matt frowned. He'd have sworn she was working hard to suppress some fierce emotion. 'So…there's one available, then, is there? A locum?' she said, after a small pause.

'Yes. I don't know if I've done the right thing but I mentioned your name. You're under no obligation, obviously.'

He looked at her hands lying flat on the case. Were they pressing into the leather or did he imagine tension in the long delicate fingers? While he watched she began to turn the ring on the middle finger of her right hand. He really looked at the thick gold band for the first time. A man's wedding ring? Was it just an adornment or did it have particular significance for her?

'For how long?'

Matt dragged his mind back to the conversation as she stopped fidgeting to cup one hand over the other. The move hid the plain jewellery from view.

'Depends on you and our vet, Bob Fryer. He needs to spend some time in Melbourne. His wife's down there with their son at the Children's Hospital.' He hesitated a moment. The child's condition was no secret around Garrangay and Bob would almost certainly tell her about it when he asked about the locum. 'Gary has leukaemia.'

No mistaking the sincere sympathy in her eyes when they lifted quickly to meet his. 'Oh, that must be so worrying for them. What's the prognosis?'

'Very good if the bone-marrow transplant takes. Which it should. They've found a very compatible donor.' He paused. 'Look, Bob's coming for dinner tonight to discuss the possibility of the locum with you but I wanted to give you some warning.'

'Thank you.'

He should leave it at that, let her go away and think about the position. 'You did say you're between jobs just now, didn't you?'

Her eyes flicked back to his and he had the feeling she'd been so consumed by her thoughts that she'd almost forgotten his presence.

'I am, yes.' She was silent for a moment. 'Though that's not the only consideration.'

'I suppose you have commitments in Melbourne, people to go home to, a partner?' He nearly winced at his lack of subtlety but he was still interested in the answer.

'Not…really, no.'

What did that hesitation mean? Had she just broken up with someone? Or was there someone that she didn't consider important? The way Sophie hadn't thought he and Nicky were important. He had no right to an explanation but the urge to demand one was hard to suppress.

He tried another tack. 'Are you worried about the large-animal side of the practice?'

'It's a consideration, certainly. I haven't done any since university.'

'Bob's arranged for some limited cover from a Hamilton practice so I'm sure they'd be happy to consult. And cover any days that you need off. Like the weekend.'

'The weekend?'

'The show on Saturday, though you'll possibly need to work there if you take the position.' He watched her reaction.

'Oh, yes. Nicky's event. I hadn't forgotten. Just hadn't put the two things together yet.'

'Then, there's the Grampians,' he said.

'The Grampians?'

'On Sunday. Our trip.' She *had* forgotten that. Didn't that put him in his place? So much for his interpretation of her blush and apparent tension around him this evening. Just because he was suffering these inconvenient pangs of attraction, it didn't mean the feeling was mutual.

Still, she'd remembered her promise to his son about the show event and that was the most important thing. If his own ego felt a little battered, he'd get over it.

'Oh, of—of course.' Her fingers tightened around her folder briefly before she stood. 'Thank you for telling me about the job, Matt. I'll think about it. See you later, then.'

He smiled tightly. Would she accept the position? He was no closer to knowing.

And no closer to knowing if he really wanted her to.

* * *

Caitlin stood from the side of her bedroom window and watched Doreen picking beans for tonight's dinner. The quiet, methodical act seemed to epitomise Doreen's love for her home and family.

Each night so far, Caitlin had been invited to share the evening meal with them. She loved being a part of their unit. Even as an outsider, looking in, she could feel their warmth enveloping her. Something in her spirit was desperate to be steeped in that generous, unconditional acceptance and caring. It was so different from what she'd grown up with.

At the same time, she felt torn, as though her silence about her father's death meant she was enjoying something she didn't deserve.

She closed her eyes and sighed. She was no closer to breaking the news to Doreen. And her holiday was nearly half-over.

But what if she took the locum position Matt had suggested? It was almost too good to be true. She wanted to grasp the offer with both hands. If she stayed longer, she wouldn't have to spring the sad news about Martin Brown's death on her aunt in the next few days. She'd have time. Surely, the perfect opportunity to tell Doreen about her brother would present itself.

And she could get to know Doreen better. And Nicky, too.

And, of course…Matt. Though that was potentially dangerous to her peace of mind.

The whole man-woman attraction thing had never hit her like this before. Being near him, hearing his voice, watching him with his family. All these commonplace things left her weak and vulnerable. Afraid of the impact he had on her senses.

But surely familiarity would take care of that. She just had to keep control until her mind and body became accustomed to him. It would happen soon…she would make sure of it.

CHAPTER EIGHT

CAITLIN had decided to stay.

Good thing or bad?

On the morning of the show, two days later, Matt was still undecided. He rubbed soap into a grubby mark on Nicky's buff jodhpurs.

Doreen had deserted him to take her prize roses in for judging. Caitlin was still around somewhere; she'd drifted in for coffee and toast while he prepared Nicky's breakfast. He huffed out a sigh and looked up at the clock.

'Nicky? Are you nearly ready?'

'Da-ad! I can't *do* it.' Nicky stomped to the laundry door, bottom lip wobbling alarmingly. The bridle, so easy to take apart last night, was still a jumbled assortment of leather and metal dangling from his hands.

'Give me a minute to finish this.' Matt stamped on the urge to point out he'd been against dismantling the fiendishly complicated apparatus in the first place. But Nicky had insisted it needed to be cleaned *everywhere*. 'Then I'll see what I can do.'

As he rinsed the fabric free of suds Caitlin appeared, coffee-mug in hand,

'Here, now, let me see what you're about.' She put the mug on top of the clothes drier then crouched beside Nicky.

Matt watched his son's distress melt away as she wove the straps and buckles magically into order.

'Do you think you'll be able to come an' watch me today, Caitlin?'

'I do, yes,' she murmured as she slipped the last strap into place then handed the bridle to Nicky.

'It'll be harder for you now 'cos you're working an' you've got responsibilities an' stuff.'

He was trying to be so grown up about the possible disappointment that Matt's heart went out to him.

'I have, but I'm sure I'll manage.' She grinned at Nicky. 'Are you too old for a good-luck kiss, then?'

'Nope.'

She planted a kiss on each of the boy's pink cheeks. Matt was debating whether he could reasonably suggest he could do with some Irish luck, too, when she glanced at her watch.

'I must run.' She rose smoothly to her feet, bending quickly to pop a kiss on Nicky's forehead. 'For extra luck.'

'Caitlin?' Matt wanted her to look at him, too.

She paused with her hand on Nicky's shoulder. 'Yes?'

'Thank you.' Matt gestured at the bridle. 'You've saved us a major tantrum. Probably mine.'

'My pleasure.' Her smile temporarily erased the wariness she'd treated him with over the last few days. 'You'd have managed fine if it hadn't had a caverson noseband.'

'Er, right.' Matt watched her go, aware that Nicky was doing the same. The Gardiner males had it bad.

'She likes me.' His son beamed up at him when they were alone again.

Matt grinned. 'She does indeed.'

'She likes you, too, Dad.' The look Nicky had given him held a knowing gleam far beyond his years.

Was it against the rules of parenting for a father to interrogate a nine-year-old about a possible love interest?

'Why do you say that?' It was a struggle to sound uninterested, but Matt thought he managed fairly well.

''Cos.'

Nothing profound there. He was conscious of sharp disappointment.

Unfortunately, a handful of casual questions later he was no closer to understanding what Nicky had seen or felt.

Springtime in the Australian bush. Was there anything more beautiful? And for now she belonged, at least temporarily, as the Garrangay veterinary locum. Caitlin didn't want to pinch herself lest she *did* wake up and find that she wasn't assessing a patient at the local A and P show.

She loved it all. The smell of sweaty, snorting horses, the rhythmic pounding of hooves as they trotted and cantered by.

Sun warmed Caitlin's back as she suppressed a smile and watched the walking gait of a lean bay thoroughbred.

'He's certainly stepping short on that hind leg, Robyn.' She ran her hand over the hock down to the fetlock. No swelling or heat in the limb. With the hoof balanced on her thigh, she applied careful pressure to the sole with a pair of pincers. When she reached the toe, the animal pulled back, wrenching the hoof out of her grasp.

'He's very tender in the toe area. We need to get his shoe off to have a closer look.'

'I guess that's the end of riding him today,' Robyn said, resigned. 'What do you think the problem is?'

'Could be seedy toe or—' A flash of wild movement caught Caitlin's eye. She spun to see a solid grey hack galloping towards a large practice jump. Arms flapping, the rider urged on the heedless flight.

'Oh, no. He's going too fast,' gasped Robyn, confirming Caitlin's fears. 'That's John Meredith on his new horse.'

With its head carried so high, Caitlin wondered if the horse was even aware of the obstacle in its path. Her breath caught in her throat, she reached for the radio at her belt and waited the suspended seconds to see if disaster would be averted.

Suddenly, hindquarters bunched, the horse twisted and

swerved, pitching the rider headfirst into the poles. As the poles clattered to the ground Caitlin began running, the radio held close to her mouth.

'Dr Gardiner to the exercise area urgently. Possible spinal injury to adult male rider.'

'Be right with you, Caitlin.' Matt's voice was calm. 'Keep him as still as possible.'

The spooked animal scrambled away, dragging the boy's frighteningly inert body for several paces before his foot slipped free of the stirrup.

Other spectators that were closer began to unfreeze and converge on the victim.

'Don't move him,' Caitlin called as she reached them.

'I was just going to take off his helmet,' a woman said, her hand on the chinstrap.

'Let's leave it until we see how badly he's hurt.' On her knees, Caitlin leaned over and touched the boy's shoulder and spoke firmly. 'Can you hear me, John? I want you to open your eyes for me.'

After a moment the lashes fluttered and clouded brown eyes stared up blankly.

'That's good, John. I want you to keep very still for us. Can you understand me?'

Apart from blinking slowly, he made no response.

'Should we call First Aid or something?' said the woman opposite Caitlin.

'Dr Gardiner's on his way.' Caitlin smiled reassuringly at her then moved to kneel at the boy's head, placing her hands on either side of his helmet. 'The best thing we can do is keep John as quiet as we can until he gets here.'

'Is he going to be all right?'

'I'm sure he'll be fine. Do you know if he's at the show with anyone?'

'His parents will be here. I've seen their alpacas in the pavilion.'

'Could you find them? They'll want to know what's happened.' As the woman rose to leave, Caitlin added, 'Perhaps have them paged if you have trouble locating them.'

Turning her attention back to the boy on the ground, Caitlin was pleased to see his eyes were still open and he seemed to be breathing comfortably. She couldn't see any obvious injuries apart from his reduced state of consciousness.

'John, you've had a fall.' That slow blink again as though her voice was registering on some level. 'The doctor's on his way to see you. He'll not be long.'

The circle of onlookers shuffled back.

'Matt!' Try as she may, she couldn't quite stifle the relief in her voice. Collecting herself quickly, she described the accident. 'He obeyed when I asked him to open his eyes but other than that he's not responding.'

'Okay, good. And you've kept his head stabilized. Well done. I want to get him into a cervical collar before we look at anything else. If I hold his head, do you think you can ease the helmet off?'

'I can, yes.'

Matt positioned his hands on either side of the boy's face and neck, moving his fingers up as she slowly slipped the hard hat away.

'Great. I'll get you to hold him steady again.' He slipped the collar into place and fastened it.

Caitlin sat back on her heels and watched Matt work. Now that he was in charge she could acknowledge how shaken she'd been by the accident. But there was something steadying about the methodical way he assessed John, checking his vital signs, feeling for injuries. John moaned slightly as Matt removed his elastic-sided boots.

Caitlin realised the youth was looking up at her, his eyes much clearer. 'Hello, John. Are you back with us, then? I'm Caitlin and this is Dr Gardiner. We're looking after you.'

'Where...am I?'

Matt moved up alongside their patient. 'Hi, John. Do you remember what happened?'

'I remember going to the show.'

'That's right, mate. You've had a bit of a tumble. Have you got any pain?'

'My...back.'

Matt flicked his small torch expertly into John's eyes again. 'Is the pain up high around your chest or down lower?'

'Down...lower.' John gasped, his hands clenching into fists and tried to point to the area.

'Don't try to move.' Matt's voice was gentle. 'How bad is it?'

'Pretty bad.'

'Okay, hang in there. I'll give you something to help in a minute. Can you wriggle your toes for me?' When nothing happened, Matt reached down to rub his hand over each foot. 'Can you feel that?'

'Yeah.'

'That's fine, John. I'm going to give you something for the pain.' Matt's long fingers worked deftly to set up an IV cannula in John's arm. 'Can you hold this for me, Caitlin?'

'Got it.' She took the fluid bag.

Matt attached the line and set the drip rate. After popping open a morphine vial, he drew up the contents and then slowly injected it into the valve. 'This should help in a minute, mate. Is anyone at the show with you?'

'Mum...and Dad.'

'I've sent someone to get them,' said Caitlin.

'Terrific.'

'Here comes Cathy Meredith now,' said someone in the crowd.

Matt stood up. 'I want a quick word with her, Caitlin. Will you be right here for a couple of minutes?'

'Of course.'

His eyes smiled his approval. 'Yell if there's a problem.'

Caitlin looked down at John as Matt strode away. 'Did you hear that? Your mum's on her way.'

'Yeah.' The boy's voice was rough with emotion.

'It's okay, John. She'll be here soon. Just keep as still as you can now.'

A few moments later, Matt was back with a subdued-looking woman obviously trying to put a brave face on her anxiety. John's face crumpled and tears trickled out of the corners of his eyes as his mother knelt beside him and stroked his forehead.

'Hello, sweetie. Dr Gardiner tells me you've had a fall.'

'An air ambulance helicopter is on its way,' murmured Matt, coming to stand beside Caitlin. 'We're sending him straight down to Melbourne. Even if this is just spinal bruising I want him to be with the experts. Are you right to be here for a bit longer?'

'Sure.' She looked up. The glowing approval in his eyes filled her with warmth.

'Let's finish getting him set up.' Matt put his hand on Cathy's shoulder. 'Cathy? We need to get John strapped onto the board now. Can you hold his IV bag for us?'

'Oh. Yes. Of course.' Cathy scrambled to her feet and moved aside.

Caitlin smiled reassuringly as she handed her the bag.

'How are you doing, John?' asked Matt as he crouched. 'How's the pain now?'

'Okay. Better.'

'Great. We're going to strap you onto a board to hold you nice and still so we can move you.'

'Okay.'

For the first time, Caitlin realised two uniformed first-aid men were standing patiently nearby, holding a long board.

Matt signalled them into position and crossed John's arms over his chest. 'We're going to roll you onto your side, John. You might feel a bit uncomfortable but I don't want you to try to help us. Let us do all the work. Okay, mate?'

'Okay.'

Matt looked at Caitlin and the others. 'I want to check him for injuries once we've got him on his side. You're right to support his head, Caitlin?'

'I am, yes.'

'Okay, on my call. One, two, three, roll.'

Working together, they soon had John positioned on the board. As Matt fastened the straps Caitlin could hear the steady drone of an approaching helicopter.

'We'll have you on your way in a few minutes, John,' said Matt.

As Caitlin moved back, the radio at her belt crackled into life, asking her to report to the main pavilion.

'I have to go,' she said, putting her hand onto Cathy's shoulder and rubbing lightly. 'Good luck, John. I'll see you later, Matt.'

A couple of hours later, Matt made his way through the amusements area, enjoying the tinny carnival tunes, the clatter of mechanical pulleys, the screams of delicious terror. Perhaps he could talk Caitlin into a ride in the House of Horrors. The girls always squealed and clung to the nearest person when the skeleton swung out of the rafters. If Caitlin was made of sterner stuff, he'd happily cling to her.

Oh, yeah. He grinned. The thought of holding her close was *very* appealing.

He'd had a busy morning. Fortunately, nothing nearly as dramatic as John Meredith's fall. A call to the hospital had reassured him that John's scans showed no obvious fractures. He'd be kept in until he regained full mobility but it seemed likely that the boy had escaped with swelling and soft-tissue damage. Damage that would heal.

Caitlin would be pleased. She'd been brilliant at the scene, taking charge of the situation until he'd arrived, organising someone to fetch John's parents. He'd almost forgotten what a pleasure it was to work in a well-coordinated team.

He glanced at his watch.

Half an hour until Nicky's event. Would Caitlin remember her promise to be there? Part of him wanted to find her and make sure she didn't forget, didn't disappoint his son. He knew first hand the heartbreak of an adult's broken promises. Before Doreen had rescued him all those years ago, he'd had a steady diet of them from his own mother. He'd do anything to protect his son from that pain.

Matt grimaced slightly. Sure, his main concern was for Nicky, but there was a strong element of self-interest. He didn't want to be disappointed either, for her to be less than the person he wanted her to be.

There was something about her. Something that made him want to touch, be touched. Her hair, her skin, her slender curves. The urge was stronger than anything he'd felt before. Was it clouding his brain and maybe his judgement?

He and Sophie had been friends through high school, then medical school. Country kids in the big smoke. The drift into matrimony had been a mistake that had destroyed their friend-ship—Sophie's infidelity had crushed him.

Though now he wondered if he'd truly loved his ex-wife. He'd certainly never experienced the flood of sensations, physical and emotional, that Caitlin sent raging through him.

He knew the chemistry of what was happening. His blood stream was overdosed with adrenalin and testosterone. Dopamine and serotonin zinged along his neural pathways.

Unfortunately, knowing *why* he felt this way didn't help. He was powerless.

Was it mutual?

He stifled a sigh. Most evidence pointed to the contrary. Though there were a few intriguing times that he'd felt an edgy nervousness about her, a sense of…anticipation almost.

Perhaps he could talk her into a bout of wild, passionate sex, relieve his inconvenient lustful needs. Once he'd moved past this hormonal overload, she might see him as the sensi-tive new-age guy that he really was.

Yeah, right, Matthew Gardiner. That's going to happen in this lifetime.

He puffed out a resigned breath. Knowing his luck, a taste would only exacerbate the problem.

He wandered down the rows of horse stalls peripherally aware of the feverish activity. Of the metallic jangling of stirrups and bits, the smell of horse sweat and leather.

Nicky had been bursting with enthusiasm about this moment for weeks. He'd started hinting about getting a pony. Riding the school horses had sufficed until now. But Christmas was looming. No prizes for guessing what would top the wish list.

When he reached the stall Nicky had been assigned there was no excited child in sight.

Instead, Caitlin was there.

CHAPTER NINE

SHE'D kept her promise!

His rush of relief made him realise just how anxious he'd been. But too quickly that feeling ebbed, leaving a gut-wrenching ache of desire.

He braced an arm on the partition between the stalls and watched her work. Her long slender legs bent slightly at the knees as she held the pony's hind leg off the ground.

Black denim pulled tautly across her backside, large pockets flattened to the curve of each buttock. The knitted fabric of her bright red T-shirt had come away from the waistband of her jeans. He could see the shallow line of her spine in the expanse of exposed creamy skin.

A loose ponytail tamed her dark curls, leaving her nape tantalising bare. A sensitive area for her? Would she murmur encouragement if he pressed his lips to the milky skin, bit gently on the smooth flesh?

What would happen if he scooped her up and laid her on the stack of straw bales at the back of the stall? What would happen if he followed her down, matching his body to the length of hers? It was all he could do to stop himself from groaning aloud. He clenched his jaw, looking away for a few moments until he had himself under control.

Madness to think having her stay in Garrangay was a good idea.

Madness.

He ducked under one of the ropes that clipped the pony into the stall and moved closer.

'Caitlin?'

Her name snapped out, harsh and short. She jolted upright and spun to face him. Wide grey eyes met his as she stepped back into the pony's flank. The placid chestnut shifted its weight, catapulting her forward.

Matt reached out to catch her.

Caitlin gasped as her foot landed on a shifting surface. Lurching awkwardly, she looked down to see the grooming kit wrapped around her ankle. A split second later, she found herself plastered against the front of Matt's shirt, her hands clutching at the soft fabric as she tried to find her balance.

'Do you think we've got time for this, honey?'

She could hear the husky laughter in his voice, feel his chuckle rumbling in his chest, the warmth of his hands wrapped around her upper arms.

'Very funny, to be sure.' She tipped her head back so she could scowl at his grinning face. His body heat radiated into her, making her desperately aware of him and of her own turbulent response. 'Stop blathering like an eejit and help me up.'

'Of course.'

His hands shifted, wrapping snugly around her waist. A moment later she realised his intention and grabbed his shoulders as her feet dangled clear of the ground. The grooming kit fell off with a dull clatter. Instead of releasing her, he kept her close. She could feel her breasts flattened against his chest.

They were nose to nose, would have been touching if she hadn't arched her head back slightly. With their eyes level, she was trapped by his shimmering dark green stare.

'Is that better?'

She nearly gulped at the husky growl in his voice.

'No. Yes. No. That's not what I…' She swallowed, wrenching

her gaze away from the emerald eyes to the strong, angular bones of his face. 'Um, not what I meant. Put…put me down, please.'

'Of course.'

Her relief at his ready agreement was short-lived. The slow slide down his torso tormented her already sensitised breasts, made her aware of his solid strength. Made her aware of her needs and vulnerability. The few seconds that it must have taken for her feet to touch the ground seemed endless. Delicious torture.

She could feel the slight bunching of her T-shirt at her solar plexus where it had been pushed up. *If she could gather her wits, she would move to straighten it.* As soon as she'd completed the thought, Matt's hands moved, his fingers brushing the unbelievably sensitive skin at her waist.

She closed her eyes, feeling her shallow gasping breaths, clutching at his upper arms, as an avalanche of sensations raced through her. Her heart pounded, the hard beats shattering all hope of composure. Surely he could hear them, feel them. With the way they were standing, how could he not?

Opening her eyes, she found her gaze drawn to his mouth. He wasn't smiling any more.

Her gaze slid down, away from his face, away from the shapely fullness of his bottom lip to the column of his throat. His carotid pulse was surging just as erratically as hers was. The evidence of his susceptibility was deeply moving. She lifted her gaze, compelled to meet his.

He was closer, intent plain in his half-closed eyes.

His head tilted, angling so his mouth could meet hers. There was plenty of time to say no. She didn't want to stop him, but some small spark of sanity insisted on making an attempt at protest.

'Is this wise, Matt?' The words came out low and husky, disturbingly unlike her normal voice. Her hands flexed around his upper arms, over the solid muscle.

'Wise? No. But I don't care.'

The whisper of his breath passed over her waiting lips. Her eyelids fluttered down as his mouth settled over hers.

She'd waited for ever for a kiss like this. A tantalising invitation to get to know him better. She was utterly lost in the gentle teasing contact, time was suspended.

But then…it wasn't enough. She wanted—no, *needed*—more. She moaned softly, sliding her palms up over his shoulders and running her fingers into his short thick hair.

Pressing closer, she felt him move back until with a small bump he reached the wooden partition.

The kiss deepened, his lips sliding over hers, warm and firm and confident. His hands on her back, arms wrapping around her ribs, small delightful points of pressure as his fingers pressed into her flesh. All the while the wonderful, moist caress continued, promising excitement, hinting at greater pleasure. Her entire body hummed to the thrill of it. She felt at once energised and on the verge of fainting with pleasure.

A sudden clatter, loud and metallic, from a nearby stall ripped her out of the moment. She pulled back, desperately sucking in a chestful of air. Lord, what was she *doing*? She scrambled away to stare dumbly at Matt. The shock she felt was reflected in his dark eyes.

He stood, his back to the wall, legs braced apart. His arms stretched out towards her, the gesture almost a plea. If she wanted to, if she was brave enough, foolish enough, she could step forward, fit back into his embrace. Press her lips back to his glistening mouth. But the heady, seductive moment was gone and in its place the dousing chill of sanity.

And a split second later came a child's shriek, then a strident neigh from further away.

His hands slowly returned to his sides.

'Oh, Lord.' She backed away another step as she raised unsteady fingers to her lips, feeling their fullness and sensitivity. 'We must be gone in the head.'

He looked at her blankly. 'Sorry?'

'Daft, we must be daft.'

Despite the balmy warmth of the day, he felt almost cold where her body had been pressed against him.

He grunted, straightening away from the partition as he ran his fingers through his hair and around the back of his neck. The kiss had exploded in his brain, leaving him dazed and barely able to string coherent thoughts together.

Should he apologise? He didn't feel like it.

Caitlin touched her mouth, then snatched her hand away when she realised he was watching her. She scowled at him. 'You—you must be wondering where Nicky is.'

'Of course,' he said, his voice gravelly.

Her speedy composure felt like an insult. He wanted to see if it would hold if he dragged her back into his arms.

'He lost his number. Doreen's taken him to find another. They should be back any moment...' She glanced around. 'Any moment.'

'I'll wait.'

She looked as though she'd have liked to suggest he wait somewhere else but in the end she said, 'Right. I'll—I'll finish Sheba's feet, then.'

'Yes.' He watched as she bent to gather the scattered grooming gear. Her hands were shaking. *Not so composed after all.* Elation thundered through him.

'Caitlin?' He crouched beside her and reached for one of the brushes.

'Yes?' She kept her face averted.

He covered her hands with his, stilling her agitated movements, heard her quick indrawn breath. 'We need to—'

'Dad!'

Matt felt Caitlin's start. He released her as she pushed forward to gather the hoof pick.

Rising smoothly to his feet, he turned to face Nicky and Doreen. His son's excited chatter washed over him, filling the awkward void, giving him something to concentrate on. An anchor in a world turned inside out.

* * *

That evening Caitlin listened to Nicky regale them again with his third placing in his riding event. His delight with his success was engaging…and a blessing. If the dinner conversation had relied on her, the table would have been uncomfortably quiet. Especially since Matt was hardly making an effort to contribute his share either.

She pushed a piece of pumpkin around at the edge of her plate then sneaked a quick look at him, only to find him watching her. His brooding expression sent a hard jolt through her system. Was he thinking about their kiss? If so, it seemed to give him no pleasure.

Heat crept into her cheeks as she slid her gaze back to her plate. What was wrong with her? She'd been kissed before, so why all this maidenly blushing and ridiculous tongue-tied silence? Annoyed with herself, she looked back at Matt and frowned. He smiled slightly and raised one eyebrow as though he read her frustration.

The shiver of premonition she'd had when she'd first met him came back forcefully. She'd felt that staying in control would be a problem around him. And the kiss had proved her point. As soon as she'd finished her meal she was going to escape to her room. Until then, she would ignore Matt Gardiner and his eyes that saw too much.

Wrenching her gaze away from him, she was just in time to catch the puzzled look that Doreen shot between Matt and herself. Did her aunt suspect something? That was the last thing she wanted.

'Doreen, would you pass me the potatoes, please?' said Caitlin, blurting out the first thing that popped into her head.

'Of course, dear.'

Accepting the dish, Caitlin added another spoonful of the mash to the pile still on her plate.

'I meant to thank you earlier for your help with John Meredith, Caitlin.'

'I was glad to.' Talking about the case? That she could deal with. 'Have you heard how he is?'

'They've done scans and there's no lasting spinal damage, no internal damage.'

'That's grand. He's a lucky boy.'

'Yes. He's especially lucky that you were there this afternoon.'

Her smile felt more like a grimace but fortunately no one seemed to notice. She felt like a fake. Sure, helping with the injured boy had been real enough, it was everything else that was out of kilter. Matt's appreciative look. Doreen's warm motherliness. The way his family had folded her into their embrace.

For some reason, Matt's kiss had underlined how unworthy she was to be so accepted. They didn't know she was here to bring them grief.

As she worked her way doggedly through her meal, she lectured herself on the folly of being sidetracked. She needed to take back control, keep Matt at a distance. And, with her up-bringing and nomadic family, wasn't keeping her distance in relationships something she was good at?

The snippet of self-awareness was so depressing.

She was torn. There was so much here in this home, in these people, that was warm, precious, enviable.

But once she told Doreen the news about her brother, would she still be as welcome?

And if she was, would she be brave enough to reach out and try to really fit in? Wanting to belong here was different from actually carving out a niche for herself. She was afraid.

More than that.

She was terrified.

CHAPTER TEN

MATT'S kiss was the first thought that slipped dreamily into Caitlin's mind the next morning. Half-awake, she rubbed her lips over each other, reliving his taste, the feel of his mouth.

A moment later, heart thumping, she blinked her eyes wide. Oh, Lord! What had he thought when she'd backed him up against the partition? She'd behaved like a wild woman. As soon as his lips had touched hers, she'd wanted to devour him. She pulled the pillow over her hot face and smothered a heartfelt groan. She'd never reacted like that to a kiss before.

Unable to bear the trend of her thoughts any longer, Caitlin threw aside the pillow and scrambled out of bed.

A broad-brimmed raffia hat hanging on the post at the end of the bed reminded her she was spending the whole day in Matt's company.

The whole day!

How was she going to handle it after that kiss? Perhaps there'd be an emergency at the clinic. Not that she wished an injury on some poor animal.

'Get a grip, you eejit. It's not as if you're going to be alone with him.' She frowned at her reflection. Eyes shadowed with smudgy dark rings stared back, testament to her long, restless night.

'And even if you are, you've a tongue in your head. You can

say no. If you're asked. Which you won't be. Not with his family and Nicky's friend around.'

She snatched up her clothes and stalked through to the en suite for a quick shower. After a vigorous towelling that left her skin tingling, she stepped out of the cubicle.

Matt was definitely a man who would respect a woman's wishes. She smoothed moisturiser over her face. Her fingertips lingered a moment on her bottom lip, his kiss vivid in her thoughts.

He wasn't the problem...she was.

She didn't *want* to say no.

'It was just a kiss, for heaven's sake. It meant nothing.' She yanked on lightweight green cargo pants and a cream singlet top. 'He took advantage of the moment, that's all. And what was he supposed to do, with you plastered all over his shirt and looking up at him with cow's eyes?'

She looked at herself in the mirror and scowled. 'All right. So it did mean something to you but there's no future in it. He's a man with commitments. You live in Melbourne, his place is in Garrangay. And you're not in the market for a quick fling.'

She stared at her reflection a moment longer. 'A bit of conviction wouldn't go astray.'

Smoothing on a layer of lip gloss, she continued her lecture. 'This locum has bought you extra time in Garrangay so put it to good use. Concentrate on finding a way to talk to your aunt. She's the reason you're here. Maybe, once you've done that, all these other complications will get untangled.' She looked herself straight in the eye. 'Or maybe not.'

A light tapping had her spinning to face the door, her breath frozen in her lungs.

'Caitlin?'

Blood pounded through her veins at the sound of Matt's voice. *Oh, God, could he have heard anything?* She pressed her hand to her mouth to stifle a bubble of hysterical laughter.

'Yes?' she gasped.

'Are you nearly ready? Breakfast's on the table. We should head off shortly.'

'Right. Yes.' She cleared her throat and breathed deeply to steady the quaver in her voice and tried again. 'I'll only be a moment.'

She grabbed Doreen's raffia hat, a long-sleeved cotton shirt and her bag. By the time she got down to the kitchen Matt was packing sandwiches and flasks and water bottles into knapsacks. Her treacherous heart skipped a handful of beats as her eyes drank in the sight of him.

'Caitlin, dear, did you sleep well?' Doreen didn't wait for an answer, which was just as well since the power of speech deserted Caitlin as soon as Matt's eyes met hers. Caitlin made a noncommittal sound as she crossed quickly to the table and slid into a chair.

'Try this marmalade. It's made with mandarins.'

'Thank you.' Caitlin took the proffered dish from her aunt and scooped out some of the chunky orange spread. 'Looks delicious,' she said, before biting into a slice of toast.

'It won first prize in the jam section at last year's show.' Doreen smiled and picked up her cup. 'Have you recovered from yesterday? You had such a busy day with Matt.'

Her aunt didn't know the half of it, thought Caitlin, coughing to dislodge a toast crumb that threatened to choke her. Though she tried not to let it, her gaze flicked back to Matt, to find him watching her with a slight smile. She swallowed and turned her attention back to her breakfast.

'I'll put these in the car and get Nicky and his friend David ready. There's an extra water bottle here for you, Caitlin.'

'Thank you.'

Caitlin hurriedly finished her last mouthful and walked out to the front porch with Doreen. The four-wheel-drive was parked in front of the house.

'Enjoy yourselves and take care,' called Doreen from the porch.

'We will.' Matt opened the tailgate of the vehicle and stacked the rucksacks on the floor.

'You're not coming?' Dismayed, Caitlin stopped at the bottom of the steps and looked up at her aunt.

'Gracious, no, dear,' answered Doreen. 'All that hiking is too much for me these days.'

'Oh.' Caitlin bit her lip. How thoughtless. She should have realised the day might be too strenuous for someone with angina. 'I could stay and keep you company.'

'Nonsense, I wouldn't hear of it. You'll have a lovely time with the boys.'

Caitlin looked over her shoulder. Matt stood at the side of the vehicle, watching and waiting.

Nicky leaned out of the back window. 'C'mon, Caitlin.'

She lifted a hand in acknowledgement. 'Are you sure, Doreen?'

'Absolutely. Off you go. I'll look forward to hearing all your adventures when you get back.'

Caitlin turned and walked around to where Matt held the door open. He moved slightly when she reached him and her footsteps faltered. She looked up to find his green eyes focused solemnly on her face.

'If I promised not to bite, would you relax?' His voice was pitched low so only she could hear.

She tightened her grip on the brim of her hat and looked at him steadily. 'As I recall, it's not your bite that's the problem.'

His gaze settled on her mouth and Caitlin's pulse jumped. 'If I promised not to kiss you, would you relax?'

'And *do* you?'

'Promise not to kiss you?' His eyebrow climbed. She could almost see the cogs turning in his mind. 'If I must.'

'You…must.' But a small thrill raced along her nerves. He sounded as though he wanted to kiss her.

'Then, I…will.' He gave her a teasing grin. 'Enjoy the day, Caitlin.'

She nodded, a confusing mix of emotion churning in her stomach. Relief. But surely it wasn't disappointment. How contrary could she be?

Once they were on their way, Matt set himself to be entertaining, regaling her with stories about the area. History, people, fauna, flora, activities.

The road undulated through the valley. Vegetation—gum trees, banksias and tea tree—grew close to the road, with breaks in the foliage affording glimpses of the towering rock buttresses of the Grampians.

'If you're feeling brave, we could try abseiling or rock climbing,' said Matt.

Caitlin turned to look at him. 'Are you joking?'

'No. Why?'

'No way will you get me to do such a thing.' She laughed and realised, with a sense of surprise, she was enjoying herself. 'It's a mystery to me why people do.'

'Not a thrill seeker, then?'

'Life dishes up enough thrills without having to look for them like that, don't you think?'

'It's good for us to get out of our comfort zone occasionally.' He looked at her, only the briefest glance as he was driving. His eyes were warm, sparkling with humour, enveloping her in a bubble of intimacy.

Didn't he realise she was out of her comfort zone right now?

'I don't need to dangle at the end of a flimsy rope to feel that way,' she muttered.

'Really?' He sounded intrigued.

'Is it something you enjoy yourself? Rock climbing?' she asked hurriedly.

'I…haven't done any for a long time but, yes, I used to enjoy it.' There was a wistful note in his voice and she wondered why he'd given it up.

'I'll watch from level ground with the boys if you want to

try some today.' Though she wondered how she'd feel seeing him swinging from a rope halfway up a dangerous rock face.

'Would you?' Pursed lips and a small frown suggested he was mulling the idea over. 'Another time perhaps. Today I'll settle for a walk before lunch.'

In a small car park, half an hour later, he handed Caitlin her backpack. 'We probably won't need these but it's always a good idea to be prepared. This walk will take us about an hour and a half.'

'We're going to earn our lunch, then.' She glanced up at him, her eyes shining and her beautiful lush mouth curved.

He'd promised not to kiss her—but he hadn't promised not to want to. He turned back to the vehicle, staring blindly into the back as he struggled to quell the sudden need to reach for her.

'Matt?'

'We can skip this if you'd prefer. There's plenty of other sightseeing to do.' The words came out harsher, more impatient, than he'd intended. He glanced at her.

There was a moment of silence and her face fell. 'Think I'm a wimp, do you?' Her voice was light but he detected a note of hurt beneath the banter. 'Don't think I'm up to a *wee* bit of a walk?'

He shrugged uncomfortably, lifting the boys' backpacks out and shutting the tailgate. 'It's a bit more than a wee walk, Caitlin.'

'There's a challenge if ever I heard one.' She lifted her chin slightly. 'Let's get to it, shall we?'

He watched as she slipped her pack onto her shoulders and set off. Nicky and David came racing back to him for their backpacks and scampered after her. Shouldering his own burden, he followed more slowly, his thoughts centred on Caitlin's words.

Was she right? Was he setting a task, a challenge for her?

Sophie had only been here with him once. She hadn't been

interested, hadn't understood his fascination with the mountain range, and after a while he'd stopped asking her to come. He'd rationalised the time apart as a sign of a healthy relationship. No jealousy or fretting. Of course, he hadn't realised that Sophie had found her own entertainment.

Perhaps, deep down, he did hope Caitlin would fail so he could find reasons to distance himself from her. Or was he hoping she'd succeed, so he could give himself permission to fall for her?

But getting involved again meant putting himself on the line, trusting his ability to make good choices. Was he ready to do that yet? He didn't know the answer.

Quick strides soon brought him close enough to appreciate the gentle sway of her hips as she walked easily along the track. The boys gambolled happily around her and Matt smiled at their antics.

He huffed out a small sigh. Permission to distance himself from her? Who was he kidding? He was well past being able to do that easily.

CHAPTER ELEVEN

'TELL me what a nice Irish girl like you is doing in a place like this.'

The question wrenched Caitlin out of her daydream. She pulled her attention from the bold magpie eyeing her from a few feet away back to the man lounging on the picnic rug beside her. Matt had moved even closer, she realised. Propped up on one elbow, he watched her, his eyes alight with curiosity.

Her heart began an uncomfortable jig.

'You invited me,' she said, hoping her voice didn't betray her sudden attack of nerves.

'So I did.' He smiled lazily. 'But I meant in general rather than today specifically.'

'I see.' Her mind spinning over a dozen different answers, she leaned forward to pour more coffee into her cup. A distraction was what she needed. 'Would it surprise you to know my birth certificate's as Australian as yours?'

'You were born in Australia?'

'I was, yes.' The tangent she'd chosen wasn't the diversion she'd have wished. Followed to its source, it was far too close to why she was in Garrangay in the first place. A Freudian slip perhaps? *Think of something else, a safer topic.* She lifted the Thermos again and gestured at his cup. 'Want some more coffee?'

'Yes, thanks.' He held out his mug, his long fingers wrapped around the dark blue acrylic. 'But you were brought up in Ireland?'

She watched the level of dark brown liquid rising as she poured carefully then screwed the lid back on the flask before answering. Bless the lingering traces of her accent. A much better direction for their conversation. 'I was brought up in many places. But I spent a lot of time in an Irish boarding school.'

'Boarding school? What was that like?'

A lonely, frightening banishment for a child's ill-conceived rebellion. But she couldn't say that and ultimately she'd thrived on the stability of it. 'Effective. It turned me out at the end with what I needed to study veterinary science.'

'How old were you when you first went there?'

'Ten.'

'God, that's so young. Too young.' His gaze scoured her face before moving away to search for Nicky. The unreserved love for his son was plain to see. So sweet it pierced her to her core. She couldn't imagine him packing Nicky off to boarding school under any provocation.

'I was allowed to go a year younger than usual because I was ahead in the curriculum.' And because her mother had put pressure on the board.

His eyes came back to hers, demanding her honesty. 'You didn't mind?'

'Oh, sure I minded. At the beginning.' She'd been devastated by her mother's decision. All her promises, all her begging, hadn't changed things. 'But it gave me a good education and it was for the best in the long run.'

He was silent for a long moment. 'You said you were brought up in different places…. Did your father's job move around a lot?' he asked.

Caitlin shook her head. 'My mother's. Da's job was looking after me when I was with them.' She could imagine the questions forming in Matt's mind. Family was not a subject she was ready to discuss yet, especially not questions about her father. But it would look odd if she said nothing. 'My mother is a marine scientist. She's quite well known. You might have heard of her. Rowan Butler.'

'Your mother is Rowan Butler?' he said, sounding stunned. '*The* Rowan Butler who does those underwater documentaries?'

Caitlin nodded, philosophical. She didn't want to talk about her mother either.

'You travelled with her?'

'Some of the time. You could say that I grew up with a snorkel in my mouth instead of a silver spoon.' She smiled slightly. 'I've swum with most of those marine animals I helped Nicky find for his project. And sharks, too.'

His eyebrows arched. 'You've swum with sharks and you have a problem with abseiling.'

'I could swim before I could walk but I've never been able to fly.' She slanted a teasing look at him. 'And they were very well-fed sharks.'

He chuckled. 'Oh, well, that makes all the difference.'

His gaze shifted back to where the boys were playing. 'You had an unusual childhood.'

'I did, yes.'

'Any brothers and sisters?'

She swirled the liquid in her cup. 'No. Just me.'

'It must have been lonely at times, always moving.' Had he leaned closer? The atmosphere seemed even more intimate.

'Yes.' She sipped her coffee. Her heart swelling at his unexpected understanding. 'Most people don't think of that, though. They see the glamorous parts. They don't see that there's no chance to put down roots.'

A small silence settled between them, broken by children's laughter and a distinctive bell-like native bird call. Why was she telling him all this? She didn't want his pity.

'But then I'd be the envy of everyone at boarding school

after the holidays when I came back with tales of exotic lands and fabulous sea creatures.' She set her half-empty cup aside and busied her hands gathering up the plates and utensils from lunch.

With the implements in her hand, she paused for a moment. 'I made some good friends at school, spent some holidays at their places. They had *normal* pets like cats and dogs and budgies. And horses, of course. That's where I started gathering my vast equine knowledge.'

He tilted his head. 'Jim Neilson would be impressed.'

'Wouldn't he, though.' She laughed softly, remembering her first day, her meeting with Matt. Only a week ago. It seemed hard to believe how much he'd become part of her daily existence. Even harder to believe she'd let that happen.

'You weren't tempted to follow in your mother's footsteps?' Matt's question interrupted her thoughts.

She tried for a casual shrug. 'She's...very dedicated. A tough act to follow.' She fiddled with the lid to one of the plastic containers. 'Nothing gets in the way of her work. The world needs people like her but they can be very hard to live up to.'

The lid finally snapped into place.

After a moment, Matt said, 'I'm sure she's very proud of you.'

She dropped the container into a rucksack, remembering the last time she'd seen her mother. *Proud* didn't describe the response to Caitlin's career choice. Not at all. 'I think I disappointed her when I chose to specialise in small-animal practice with domestic animals. There is so much endangered wildlife that needs to be studied, saved.'

Her words sat between them, more revealing than she'd intended. She glanced at Matt to find him looking at her, his eyes warm and sympathetic. Oh Lord, he *did* feel sorry for her.

'She sounds like Nicky's mother.' He sat up, resting his forearms on his knees, his hands loosely clasped. 'Sophie's in a research lab in Melbourne. I know she's doing important work, but sometimes I'd like her to put Nicky first.' His lips curved in a rueful smile as he lifted a hand to wave away a persistent fly. 'Nicky seems to take it in his stride. I'm the one that gets bent out of shape about it. I hate the idea he's so low on his mother's priorities.'

The far-away look on his face held sadness as well as resignation. It was all Caitlin could do to resist the urge to reach out and touch him. She picked up her coffee instead.

'He has you, Matt. And Doreen. People who love him without reservation, who do put him at the top of their priorities. I think that's the most important thing.'

He looked at her steadily as though considering her words. 'You had your father. Was it enough?'

There was a small, almost expectant pause.

'I had Da, yes,' she said slowly. 'But I wasn't his top priority. He was very much in love with my mother. And she was in love with her work. I didn't realise how much until he got sick. There was no suggestion that she would drop everything to be with him.' She tilted her head, scanning the cloudless blue sky visible through the leafy canopy of the gum tree behind them. Talking brought back the difficult months of her father's illness. But now that she'd started to bare her pain and turmoil she couldn't seem to stop the words.

'The sad thing is that Da didn't expect her to come back. I was angry for him.' She picked up a gum nut in her free hand, rolled it along her fingertips absent-mindedly. 'And maybe I was angry *with* him that he didn't expect it.'

Why had she said that? She'd barely admitted it to herself, she realised, flicking the seed pod away. Now she'd told someone else. Such unguarded confidences were uncharacteristic and…unnerving. She wondered what she might divulge next. Her father's death and her secrecy about it weighed heavily on her mind. So much so that she was compelled to this dangerous flirtation at the edges of her concealment, almost as though she was daring herself to go further.

She stared at the dregs of her drink.

'Caitlin—'

'Do you suppose Doreen put something in this coffee?' She spoke quickly to cut off whatever he'd been going to say.

He glanced at her mug, obviously confused by her change of subject. 'Like what?'

'Oh, you know…an enormous dollop of sodium pentothal perhaps? I can't believe I've blathered on like this.' She half frowned, half smiled at him as she tried to make light of their conversation. 'You're much too easy to talk to, Matt Gardiner.'

'Good.' He held her gaze for a long silent moment. Caitlin caught her breath at the unmistakable warmth she saw in the green depths. 'I want to know everything about you, Caitlin. I want to know what makes you tick.'

An odd thrill of fear and longing trickled through her. If he did know what made her tick, would he like what he found?

'Sure, and why would you? There's precious little to know.' She began stacking the used picnic utensils and containers. 'I'll pack up here if you want to go and kick the ball around with Nicky and David.'

'Trying to get rid of me?'

'Not at all,' she said, determined to ignore the pout that made his mouth look so tempting. 'I—'

'Somebody, help! Please!' Screams shattered the afternoon quiet. Caitlin looked towards the end of the picnic ground as a girl ran out of the bush. 'My boyfriend's been bitten by a snake.'

Matt rose swiftly to his feet, scooping up his knapsack as he moved. He loped towards the hysterical girl as two youths staggered into the open area behind her, one obviously supporting the other.

Caitlin followed a bare second or two later, aware of Nicky and David running over as well. As she approached the group, Matt was settling the victim on the ground in the shade.

'Where were you bitten?' Matt's voice was calm as he took

stock of the situation. Both the youths looked to him for guidance but the girl was still agitated.

Now that Caitlin was closer, she could see the victim's extreme pallor and the sheen of sweat on his skin. She hoped that was reaction to his fright and not a sign that he'd walked a long distance with venom pumping through his system.

The boy lifted one hand and flapped vaguely towards his feet.

'On his leg. On his leg. By the ankle. See?' gasped the girl, her voice rising with each word as she pointed to the expanse of bare athletic legs between the bottom of the board shorts and a pair of rubber thongs. 'Oh, God. Andrew, please don't die.'

Matt turned the leg slightly and Caitlin could see two red lines, more like shallow grazes than puncture wounds. He opened his rucksack and took out two rolls of crêpe bandage.

'Please help him. Don't let him die.'

'Jodie!' The boy groaned a faint protest.

'Andrew, is it?' asked Matt. The boy nodded. 'I'm Matt Gardiner. I'm a doctor. You're going to be fine.'

Matt's concentration was focussed on his patient and he continued speaking in a soothing tone. 'I'm going to strap your leg. I want you to sit quietly, concentrate on relaxing. Deep breaths now.'

'Why aren't you putting on a tourniquet? What are you doing? What's he doing?' Jodie was nearly screaming. 'Oh, God, we need a tourniquet.'

Her hysteria flowed out in a swamping tide, raising everyone's tension. Matt had his hands full with the bite victim.

Caitlin grasped Jodie by the shoulders, turned her so her back was to her boyfriend.

'Jodie! Look at me!' Caitlin pitched her voice to a hard, no-nonsense edge. Tremors ran through the body beneath her hands but it stopped trying to pull away. 'Jodie. Listen to me. Andrew is *not* going to die.' The panicked gaze focussed on her and the hiccuping sobs quieted for a crucial moment. 'Dr. Gardiner is putting on a pressure bandage.'

'Your—your husband's a—a doctor?' she said, between gulps.

'He is, yes,' said Caitlin, not bothering to correct the mistake about her relationship to Matt. 'Andrew's in good hands. Once the pressure bandage is on, we'll get him to hospital.'

It would have been better if they hadn't moved their friend. The mad dash into the picnic area might have increased the danger considerably.

'I need you to take a deep breath now, Jodie, and keep calm,' said Caitlin, keeping steady eye contact and continuing to speak in a no-nonsense manner. 'You can help by answering some questions for us. Can you do that for us?'

'Y-yes.'

'Good girl.' She rubbed the still quivering shoulder. 'How far do you think Andrew walked after he was bitten?'

'Not—not far. We were just over there.' She turned and pointed to the nearby bush.

'Only about ten feet,' said the second boy, confirming Jodie's story. 'That's why Andy was trying to pick the snake up. Because it was so close to the picnic area.'

Caitlin suppressed a sigh. The boy's intention had been commendable but the outcome predictable. Most snake bites happened when people interfered with the naturally shy creatures. 'Do you know what type of snake it was?'

'It was dark brown,' said Andrew, through lightly chattering teeth.

'Any stripes, colour variations?' asked Matt.

'I don't know,' said Jodie, when Andrew shrugged. 'I didn't really see all that clearly. Andy was the one closest to it. Is it important?'

'Should we go and look for it?' asked the second boy.

'No!' Caitlin spoke at the same time as Matt. She shared a quick, speaking glance with him.

'No, don't worry,' said Caitlin more calmly. The snake was probably long gone but they didn't want to risk a second bite victim. 'The hospital can do a kit test. Jodie, why don't you hold Andrew's hand while I help Matt?'

Jodie wiped her cheeks and sniffed before going to sit beside her boyfriend to stroke his arm. If the girl's smile was a little shaky she at least held her tears at bay.

'Do you need something for a splint, Matt?' Caitlin examined the neat bandaging.

'I've got a couple in the back of the car. Could you grab those?' He tore open the next packet and continued strapping the limb.

'Keys?'

'In the front of my rucksack,' he said, pointing with his chin. 'Bring some more bandages, too, please. You'll find them in the grey box. And a blanket. And put a call through to Emergency Services while you're there, please, Caitlin. Let them know they'll need to test for the toxin. We don't know what sort of snake but the bite area hasn't been washed.'

'Sure.'

Though they were wide-eyed and fascinated with proceedings, Nicky and David managed to tear themselves away to follow her back to the vehicle.

'He looks real sick, Caitlin. He's not gonna die, is he?' asked Nicky in an awed voice, when she'd made the phone call.

'I'm sure Andrew will be just fine. Your dad knows what he's doing.' She unlocked the back door. 'Andy's had a nasty fright so he's probably suffering from a wee bit of shock.'

'Oh,' they said in unison, sounding half relieved and half disappointed.

Caitlin suppressed a grin. She'd had very little experience with small boys but she suspected that a ghoulish fascination with injuries was probably normal.

'Would you be able to give me a hand here, boys?'

They stepped forward eagerly as she handed them each a blanket. Their sense of importance at doing something to help was almost tangible.

'What's going to happen to him?' asked Nicky, as she gathered the bandages and splints for Matt.

She locked the back of the vehicle and set off back to the group, a boy on each side.

'Well, we've got an ambulance on the way and we'll send him off to hospital. They might have to give him an injection of anti-venin,' she said. Though that came with its own set of risks. The unfortunate Andrew would probably be kept in hospital under close observation for at least twenty-four hours to see if the injection was necessary.

'That's to stop the poison, right, Caitlin?'

'It is, yes.'

A short time later the ambulance she'd called arrived and Caitlin stood to one side with Jodie and the boys while Matt handed over to the paramedics. With her arm around Jodie's blanket-covered shoulders, she watched Matt help transfer Andrew onto the stretcher.

Matt turned back to ask if Jodie wanted to ride in the ambulance. A beam of late afternoon sunshine slanted through the treetops, shining at an oblique angle directly into his eyes. Spokes of clear green radiating out from black pupils held Caitlin oddly transfixed. Her heart squeezed painfully, her breath shallow and fast.

A snapshot of the moment was imprinted on her mind. The sound of the idling ambulance engine, kookaburras laughing in the distance, the smell of eucalyptus oil in the warm air.

Then he smiled, the corners of his eyes crinkling appealingly.

A shock of hot recognition ran through her, leaving her breathless and shaken.

Numb, she helped Jodie into the back of the vehicle, accepting the return of the blanket after the paramedic had replaced it with one of theirs. She seemed to see herself from a distance, looking normal, going through the motions of accepting Jodie's thanks, wishing them luck. No sign of the sick panic she could feel building in her chest, her stomach.

With a final, strained smile she turned away and walked back to the picnic blanket, her legs feeling disjointed and rubbery.

She was lost.

How could she resist this man? In that peculiar charged moment, she'd felt there was nothing she wouldn't do to stay with him.

How could that be?

CHAPTER TWELVE

HAD it been like this for her father? No sacrifice was too much?

Caitlin began mechanically packing the picnic utensils into the basket before stowing it into the back of the vehicle.

Da had nurtured his marriage with a deep love, a giving spirit. So proud of his wife's accomplishments, he'd never questioned the demands her work had put on him, on their family unit.

Leaves and twigs flew as she gave the tartan picnic rug a vigorous shake. She folded and rolled it up.

Her parents had had such a lopsided relationship. Something she would never tolerate for herself…or so she'd thought. How woefully naive she had been to vow never to give more than she was given. As if emotion could be parcelled out that way.

A tug on her sleeve snapped her out of her thoughts. Nicky was looking up at her. His eyes, so much like Matt's, were filled with concern. She realised he must have spoken to her several times while she'd stood staring into space, the blanket clutched to her chest.

'Sorry, Nicky. I was away with the fairies.' She moved her mouth into a smile of reassurance. 'What was it you wanted?'

'Can we have a drink, please?'

'Of course.' She rummaged in the esky then handed them each a small fruit juice. After a hurried thank you, they darted away to continue their ball game.

She watched Nicky laughing and wrestling with his friend. He was so happy and secure. Matt, Nicky, Doreen. A real family that played and laughed together. And talked.

Today, she'd talked. Blurted out things about herself, her past, her feelings. Things that she hardly acknowledged to herself. Now she felt almost exposed, raw.

Perhaps that's why she reacted so strongly to Matt. All she needed to do was back off a little, pull herself together and she'd be okay.

Happier that she'd found a reasonable explanation for that peculiar moment of shock, she risked another look at Matt.

He stood watching the ambulance move off as he talked on his mobile phone. Probably updating the staff at the emergency unit in Stawell. Caitlin gave a small sigh of relief. There, then. She was fine. She could look at him and everything stayed where it should. No little shocks.

He was just a nice-looking man. Gorgeous, in fact.

The call finished, he slipped the phone back into his pocket and strode towards her. His body moved easily, with an economy that was a pleasure to watch.

He looked up and caught her eye, his lips curving. And everything spun out of control.

She had to find another way to handle this.

Or she was in deep, *deep* trouble.

The temptation to make her excuses, run back to Melbourne, write Doreen a letter was overwhelming. She hated being a coward. But sometimes retreat was the only sensible option.

Thankfully, she didn't need to make conversation when they got back on the road. The boys filled in the silence with their chatter in the back seat.

She concentrated on the scenery. Banksias with distinctive yellow cones, tea tree, correa. She *would* stifle the turmoil that threatened to swamp her, even if she had to identify every single plant they passed on the way home. All she needed to do was apply a bit of common sense to the situation.

That shattering moment earlier had been an aberration. She hadn't slept well last night. No wonder, with Matt's kiss playing over and over in her restless dreams. It would pass…it *had* to pass.

All they needed was some normal interaction. Though not too much of that either. He was a dangerously attractive man— someone who *would* be too easy to fall in love with. And she wasn't ready for the sort of sacrifices that would mean. She had her life mapped out. And love and commitment were comfortably down the track. Not here. Not now.

'You're very quiet.' Matt's voice jerked her out of her thoughts.

'Am I?' For the life of her she couldn't think of an intelligent response.

'Tired?'

'A little. I was thinking…' She couldn't possibly tell him what was really on her mind. A burst of laughter from the back seat gave her a safe escape. 'Thinking it'd be good to harness the boys' energy.'

Matt chuckled. 'Hard to believe they've run around all day.'

'Yes.'

'Nicky should sleep well tonight.'

'So should I,' said Caitlin, then immediately wished she could unsay the words. They seemed to reverberate in the conversational lull, reminding her again of why she was so tired. 'Not that I'm saying I didn't sleep well last night.'

That was *worse*. Cheeks burning, she turned to look out the window.

'I didn't,' Matt murmured. She darted a quick look at him and caught his cheeky smile. 'Sleep well, that is.'

'Really?' *Matt in bed.* Just what she didn't need to think about. She cleared her throat. 'Well, um, you should tonight.'

'Perhaps.'

'Are we nearly home, Dad?' Caitlin was glad of Nicky's interruption.

'Not far.'

'Can Davey come back and play?'

'Not tonight.'

'Ple-ease?' He stretched the word out as though that might make it harder to resist. Caitlin hid a grin.

'No. It's getting late and you've both got school tomorrow.'

'But, Da-ad.'

Matt stifled a sigh and hoped this wasn't going to turn into a protracted argument. 'No, Nicky.'

'Not even for a little while?'

'Not even for a little while,' said Matt firmly.

The boys made their reluctant farewells at David's house a short time later. Matt looked at his son's glum face before glancing at Caitlin. Her eyes held a mixture of sympathy and laughter. He smiled wryly. It was nice to share the little parenting moment.

He restarted the car and headed for home. Today had been…great. A companionable silence filled the vehicle and his thoughts centred comfortably on the woman beside him. She was *fun*, fitting in with him and Nicky in a way that Sophie had never wanted to.

He slowed and moved to the left as a large articulated truck approaching them strayed over the centre line. A flash of white shot beneath the wheels. Matt instinctively jammed on the brakes. Hands gripping the steering-wheel, he waited for a thump.

Nothing happened.

He checked the rear-view mirror. The only vehicle on the road was the disappearing truck.

'Everyone all right?' He slowly pulled over to the side of the road then reached for his seat-belt buckle. 'Nicky? Caitlin?'

They both nodded, eyes wide.

'What happened?'

'I'm not sure. Something ran out from under the truck. We don't seem to have hit it but I just want to check.'

'I'll come, too,' said Caitlin.

'Thanks. Nicky, wait here, okay? We'll just be a minute.'

Nothing on the road. Matt was beginning to wonder if it had been a sheet of paper when Caitlin pointed. 'I've found the culprit.'

A dog peered at them from behind a small bush. One paw in the air and a mixture of hopefulness and fear plain on the little spotted face. Matt walked forward but the animal slunk a short distance away before turning to look back at them.

'Let me try.'

Caitlin approached the pup slowly, her voice soft and coaxing. Moments later, she crouched, holding out her hand for it to sniff.

'Well done. Is he hurt?'

'No, I don't think so. He's got a bit of dried blood on his back leg but it doesn't look serious. I'll wash it and check again when we get home. His condition's a bit poor.' Caitlin was checking the dog as best she could while the squirming form tried to lick her hands and face. 'I wonder how long he's been out here.'

'What do you think? Dumped?'

'Hard to say. No collar. Probably. I'll take him into the clinic and check for a microchip. He's still very young.' She sounded distracted and he could tell her mind was on the pup.

'Can we keep him, Dad?' Nicky materialised by his side. 'We can call him Spotty.'

'We'll see, Nicky.' Matt looked down into his son's hopeful face. The pup had found a champion. 'Someone might claim him.'

As soon as they arrived home, Nicky was out of the car. Caitlin smiled as she watched him heading towards the house with an armful of wriggling pup.

'We need to wash him before he gets the run of the house, Nicky,' Matt called. 'And Caitlin needs to check him again.'

'Sure, Dad.' Nicky flashed her an easy grin.

'Mum's going to be thrilled. What's the bet the laundry will be awash by the time we get inside.' Matt's voice was filled with amusement and, though she wasn't looking at him, Caitlin could tell he was grinning.

'Nothing surer.' She gathered her gear quickly and prepared to follow Nicky.

'Caitlin.' Matt's hand settled on her upper arm, stopping her escape. 'I had a good time today.'

'I—I did, too. Thank you.' She could feel the warmth of his hand through the light cotton of her shirt. She stared at his mouth, suddenly remembering the heat of their kiss. The firm, warm confidence of his lips on hers, the faint abrasiveness of his chin.

'I'm sorry we were interrupted when we were.' At her blank look, he added, 'The snake bite.'

'Oh. Yes. Well…' She shrugged. 'I—I guess it's part of your job.'

'Of both our jobs, yes. We've had a busy day.' His grin turned to something more intimate, warm and inviting. 'But I'm still sorry. I enjoyed our talk.'

Caitlin could hardly think straight with his thumb rubbing the sensitive area on the inside of her arm. How much more potent would it be on her bare skin?

'Listening to me blather on, you mean. Way too deep and meaningful.' Her voice sounded breathless and shaky to her own ears. 'I thought men avoided stuff like that.'

She knew she wasn't being fair. He was a doctor committed to his community, a loving and active father, a loyal and protective foster-son. No, not a superficial person by any yardstick.

He gave her a well-deserved look of reproach. His hand slipped down her arm to her hand.

'I'm interested in you, Caitlin.' The words came out quickly as though, if he didn't speak this minute, he might change his mind. Caitlin's heart skipped with a peculiar mix of excitement and trepidation as she waited to see what he'd say next. 'I'd

like to find out where this could go. We skipped a step or two
with the kiss yesterday but we're both adults, single and unattached.'

Should she invent a convenient boyfriend, someone to
protect her from herself? A buffer to Matt's attractiveness? Oh,
Lord, how desperate was that?

'Well, I am, anyway.' He sent her a lopsided smile. 'You're
definitely an adult…'

'And single and unattached,' she said, slowly. She shouldn't
encourage him but felt oddly helpless to resist knowing more.
'Where…where do you think this could go?'

'From my point of view, anywhere we want it to.' He sighed.
'As long as it's in Garrangay.'

Of course, he needed to stay here. What would he say if she
told him that it had already gone much too far? Whether it was
in Garrangay or anywhere else.

For a split second she was tempted to throw herself into his
arms, to confess everything she was hiding. To ask him how
to approach Doreen without causing pain.

To beg him to let her stay in his life.

To see if she could be open and loving.

She wanted to dive in but her innate caution kept her mute
for long seconds.

And then his hands moved on hers. She looked down to see
him rubbing the gold band on her middle finger. Her father's
wedding ring. Sanity swiftly returned. Everything was going
to change once she told them about her father.

No matter how much she wished otherwise, she knew she'd
never be the giving person that Matt's family deserved. She was
her mother's daughter—good at keeping people at arm's
length.

She'd come into their lives, accepted their wonderful hos-
pitality while holding a secret that would cause Doreen pain.
Caitlin knew, with her continued silence, she was also deceiv-
ing Matt. It didn't matter how well intentioned she was.

She had to push him away, at least try to minimise the harm she was doing.

'You don't know me,' she said harshly.

'I like what I do know very much.' His expression was so inviting, so hard to resist.

She pulled her hand away, feeling his reluctance to let go, missing the warmth as soon as he did release her. 'Maybe I think you're looking for something I can't give you.'

'Can't…or won't?' A muscle flexed along his jaw.

'Does it matter?'

'Yes. Are you saying the feeling between us is one-sided?'

She paused, unable to lie. If he had any idea of how deeply he affected her, he'd be even harder to deflect. Already she'd been foolish to kiss him. But a woman would have to be strong beyond belief not to be tempted by a man like Matt Gardiner.

'You know it's not. But a relationship…it's not that easy.' She shook her head as she slipped her hand out of his grasp. 'We can't always have what we want. And you're right—you do need to stay in Garrangay. I don't know if I can.'

Matt watched as she walked away. He felt flat and tired. She'd withdrawn. There had been a moment when he'd been sure she'd wanted to agree. He'd almost been able to see the struggle in her mind. But then she'd shut him out again.

Did that mean she wasn't interested…or that she was? The chemistry of their kiss, the heat between them was undeniable. But she'd wanted to deny it.

In fact, she almost seemed to be warning him off. If that's what she was doing, he didn't want to hear it. Even knowing there was a good chance she would go back to Melbourne, he still wanted to try.

And it wasn't just a flirtation that he was after any more either.

Did that make him a fool?

CHAPTER THIRTEEN

PASSING on good news was a treat, Matt reflected as he hung up the phone a couple of days later. The laboratory results on Laura Bennett's breast tumour showed it was an adenoma. Benign, no further treatment required. He'd been fairly sure it would be. The lump had been discrete and mobile on palpation but the confirmation from the biopsy was still a relief for all concerned.

He dropped the file back in the cabinet.

Time to head home.

Home. Matt sighed. Since Caitlin had moved out the previous day, *home* hadn't felt quite right. Bob's house had been empty, even if it was in the middle of renovations. And she'd claimed it'd be easier if she was there in case there was an emergency.

But he couldn't help wondering if he was the real reason she'd gone. He and his pushing for some acknowledgment of their chemistry.

Just as well she couldn't know his preferred method for dealing with his attraction to her. The one that involved them making wild, passionate love and *then* getting to know each other better.

He knew how these things were supposed to work. Friends first, then lovers and maybe, just maybe, spouses later.

But with Caitlin he'd be more than willing to fast-track the first step and to hell with all the caution that past experience had taught him.

More than willing.

Caitlin was at Mill House.

Bless Doreen and her love of feeding anyone who'd sit still long enough.

He found Caitlin sitting cross-legged on the floor of Doreen's hobby room, folders spread out around her.

He felt his mood rise as he leaned against the doorjamb and watched her for a few moments. Engrossed as she was in a newspaper cutting in her hand, she hadn't heard him come in.

Her hair was loose across her shoulders. The lustrous curls made him want to sink his fingers into her hair, to see if it was as silky as it looked. Her slender legs folded easily into the semi-lotus position. Matt grimaced. He hadn't been able to achieve that posture since primary school and never with Caitlin's apparent degree of comfort.

'You're back,' he said, sliding his hands into his pockets to stop the temptation to touch her.

Her head whipped up and she pinned him with a wide-eyed stare. 'I—not really. Just a visit.' She sounded breathless. 'Doreen invited me for dinner.'

'Sorry, I didn't mean to disturb you.' He suppressed a smile at the words as they tripped automatically off his tongue. A psychologist would find all sorts of layers of meaning in his words. The truth was he *would* like to disturb her. A lot.

She ducked her head.

He frowned. Was that moisture on her lashes?

'Caitlin? Is something wrong?'

'Nothing, no.' Her fingers began busily slotting papers back into the folder in her lap. 'Why would you think that?'

'Well, looking at other people's family trees always brings tears to my eyes,' he joked, after a small pause.

She slanted him a narrow eyed look. 'Sure, and I believe that.'

The glitter on her eyelashes must have been a trick of the light. He grinned, angling his head to see the folder she held.

'What were you reading?'

'Your mum's articles on Garrangay's pioneers, among other things,' she said vaguely.

'You're interested in all that?'

'I am, yes. Why shouldn't I be?' She sounded defensive but he couldn't imagine why she would be. 'You're not interested?'

He shrugged. 'True family doesn't always have much to do with biological links.'

Why had he said that? It stopped Caitlin's agitated movements but now she looked at him with an expression of soft sympathy, a file clutched to her chest. Pity was the last thing he wanted from her.

'I suppose not, no,' she said softly. 'Doreen said she was— that you were—that is…'

'Doreen told you that she's my foster-mother?' he said blandly.

'Yes. I'm sorry, I didn't mean to pry.' A delicate pink crept across her cheekbones as her eyes slid away from his.

'It's common knowledge.'

'In Garrangay, perhaps, but that doesn't mean you'd want me to know.' She looked back at him, her eyes dark with uncertainty.

Perhaps it was a good time to lay it all out, tell her about his inauspicious childhood. Something tightened in his chest. Sophie's attitude to his background had been subtly condescending.

What would Caitlin's be? He realised he wanted to take a chance and find out.

Before he could change his mind, he crossed to the sofa and sat down. He leaned forward and sifted through a pile of photographs until he came to one of himself and his biological mother.

It was the one Doreen had framed for him to have in his

bedroom until, one day, he'd decided he didn't need it any more. Even then, she'd kept the picture for him. After all these years, it was a shock to see the facial features he'd inherited from this stranger, his mother.

In silence, he held it out.

Caitlin took the photograph and studied it for a long moment. The woman's face was stunning, with beautiful green eyes and high cheekbones. The hollows beneath those bones were more pronounced than seemed healthy. 'Your birth mother?'

He nodded. 'She'd taken me down to Melbourne for the weekend.'

'You—you spent time with her, then?' Caitlin handed the picture back.

'Some. When she'd detoxed.' His eyes were sad. Caitlin longed to reach out, to hold and comfort. 'Till the next time she couldn't resist a fix.'

There was no bitterness in his voice, just philosophical acceptance. Matching his tone, she said, 'It must have been difficult.'

'It was. My mother, like most drug addicts, was always making promises she couldn't keep.'

'Is she…? Do you still see her?'

'She passed away years ago. Complications from hepatitis B.' He looked back at the photo and his lashes shielded his eyes, hiding his emotions. But Caitlin wondered if she could see a residue of his grief in the straight line of his mouth.

'Matt. I'm so sorry.'

His gaze lifted, the piercing green looking directly, deeply into her eyes. 'Thanks. I was lucky, though. I had Doreen and Pete, people I could rely on. Doreen gave me stability, loved me the way my mother couldn't,' he said, with touching simplicity.

The praise for her aunt made Caitlin feel at once proud and confused. What had happened between Doreen and Martin? What had been so bad that he'd turned his back on his only family? So bad he'd never mentioned his sister until his illness had been in its end stages? The words that he'd spoken with such difficulty in the days before he'd died, the apology that Caitlin was here to deliver, indicated a deeply painful trauma. Yet Doreen wasn't an unforgiving woman who held bitter grudges.

So why hadn't her father come back to Garrangay to sort things out years ago?

'Caitlin?'

She jolted back to reality and covered her start by straightening the folders on her knee. 'Yes?'

'Where did you go?'

Again the urge to confide was nearly overwhelming. She shrugged. 'Nowhere.'

'You looked sad.' He tilted his head, giving her a considering look. 'I didn't tell you this to make you sad. I told you because I don't want any secrets between us.'

Her heart squeezed sickeningly. She felt shaken, as though he'd touched her with an electric prod. Right this minute she was living a concealment and this wonderful man wanted to be open with her. She didn't deserve his trust.

'I meant what I said yesterday, Caitlin. I want to know you. And I want you to know me.'

She swallowed, wondering how she could bear this peculiar rawness that he made her feel. The words of caution she knew she should speak stayed locked in her mind.

Four days later, Matt tossed his keys onto the hall table and briefly studied his reflection in the mirror. His eyes looked as tired as they felt.

'Matt, thank goodness.'

He spun around at the sound of Doreen's breathless voice. She was hurrying down the hall towards him with a large flat box and a teetering stack of towels in her arms.

'I was just going out to set up the car but now you're home, you can take him.'

'Take who?' Matt frowned as he moved forward to take the load from her.

'What?' Her face creased with apparent confusion as she hovered beside him. 'Oh. Spotty. To Caitlin. I've just rung so she's expecting us. I don't know what's wrong with him. Oh, dear. Nicky's going to be so upset.'

'Where is he?'

'At soccer practice.'

Matt was beginning to feel as though he'd dropped into a farcical sitcom where he hadn't been told the story line. If it weren't for Doreen's obvious agitation he'd have been tempted to laugh.

'I meant, where's Spotty?' he said gently.

'In the laundry. He must have eaten something poisonous, but I can't imagine…. Nothing's been left out.'

When she turned and scurried along the hall, Matt tucked the burden under one arm and strode close behind, wondering what he'd find. Whatever it was wouldn't be good if Doreen was talking about poisoning.

'He's been so sick that I shut him in there while I got everything ready.'

Matt opened the door. It only took the briefest glance to see how ill the young Dalmatian was. Mucus drooled from his blunt black muzzle and his gangly spotted body heaved several times with the effort of trying to vomit.

'Right.' He took one of the large towels and handed the box back to Doreen. 'Put that in the back of the four-wheel drive, Mum. I'll carry him out.'

Matt wrapped the towel around the trembling dog and lifted him carefully. The robust bouncing creature of the past couple of days was gone, leaving a fragile trembling frame.

As he walked out to the car park, Matt could feel heat radiating through the thickness of the towel. *Too much? What was the normal body temperature of a dog?*

After laying Spotty in the makeshift bed, he shut the door and turned to face Doreen. She stood, her hands clutched to her chest, looking drawn and shaken.

'Have you got chest pain?' he asked sharply.

'What? Oh, just a little.' She looked away guiltily. 'It's nothing to worry about.'

'Come back inside.' Matt grasped her elbow and turned her towards the house. 'I'll get your medication.'

'No, Matt. Please. Take Spotty to Caitlin.'

'As soon as you've taken your medication and you're looking better.'

'You always were a stubborn boy.'

A few minutes later, Doreen reassured him that she was feeling fine. 'Now, go. Please.'

'You'll stay by the phone and ring if it happens again?'

'Yes, dear.'

'And rest?'

'But dinner needs—'

'I'll organise dinner when I get back.'

'But—'

'Promise me you'll rest or I won't go. Spotty will have to take his chances,' Matt said, with what he hoped was convincing ruthlessness.

'I promise. Please, hurry.' Doreen sent him an anxious look. 'Nicky's so attached to him.'

'I know. Try not to worry.' Matt dropped a quick kiss on her forehead. 'He'll be in good hands with Caitlin. I'll call you as soon as I get there.'

Her words still ringing in his ears, Matt drove towards the veterinary surgery. Nicky and the pup had become inseparable since the stray had decided to adopt them.

Doreen had become very fond of spotty, too. Matt sighed. And if he was honest, so had he. So much for the idea they were only minding the animal until someone came to claim it. He may as well get used to it—they were now a family with a dog.

Caitlin was hovering on the porch as he pulled into the veterinary clinic drive. She met him at the back of the vehicle. Moving forward as soon as the door was open, all her attention focussed on her patient.

Matt watched, feeling helpless. He was used to being the one in charge.

'There, now, puppy,' she murmured as she peeled back the woebegone dog's top lip and pressed her thumb to the gum. 'He's very pale. Any sign of bloody discharge?'

'Not that I've seen. Mum didn't say anything when she rang?'

'She didn't, no.'

Grabbing a handful of loose skin from the back of Spotty's neck, she pulled it up slightly. When she released it, the hump stayed in a bizarre deformity.

'See the way his skin stays up? Dehydration.' Her grey eyes were guarded as she stepped back to look up at him. 'Haley prepared the isolation area before she went home. Let's take him in and I'll finish examining him there.'

Matt scooped up the box and followed Caitlin around to the back door. The words 'isolation area' sent a chill of foreboding through him.

Caitlin ushered him into a small room just off the entrance hall.

Matt took a quick glance around, noting the stainless-steel table in the middle of the room. On a stand at the table's corner hung a fat plastic fluid bag, the drip line looped over the hook. A collection of instruments was laid out on a metal tray. At one side of the room stood a cage, its large grilled door open. A thick layer of newspapers covered the floor.

'On the table?'

'Thanks.'

He lifted Spotty onto the spotless surface. 'I need to make a quick call.'

'Sure.'

Matt held the pup's collar with one hand and punched the numbers into his mobile phone with the other.

The pup stood passively, head drooping, as Caitlin lifted his tail to insert a rectal thermometer.

'Mum. How are you feeling?'

'Good as gold, dear. How's Spotty?'

'Caitlin's looking at him now. Are you resting?'

'Yes, dear.' The sound of long-suffering patience was plain in her voice. 'Though I do think I could peel a few potatoes.'

'No, no potatoes,' he said firmly. 'Consider yourself grounded. I'll see you shortly.'

Concerned grey eyes met his as he disconnected and slipped the phone back into his pocket. 'Doreen's not well?'

'Angina.'

'Is—is she all right?'

'She will be if she does as she's told,' he muttered.

'You can leave Spotty with me.'

He hesitated briefly. 'I'll stay until you've finished the examination.'

She nodded and glanced at the thermometer. Matt didn't like the pensive expression on her face as she wiped the cylinder and slid it back into a fluid-filled jar. Meeting his eyes as she rested her hands on the dog's shoulders, Caitlin said, 'I'd like to run a test to confirm it but Spotty has classic symptoms of Parvo.'

'And that's bad?' He could tell by the sombre look on her face but he had to ask the question anyway.

'It is, yes. I vaccinated him on Monday when I brought him in for a check over but it's too soon for him to have developed effective immunity.' One of her long, delicate hands stroked the dog's short coat.

Matt watched the gentle rhythmic movements as he considered her diagnosis.

'We'll start him on a fluid drip and a course of antibiotics,' she said, breaking into his thoughts. 'The virus damages the intestinal wall and we don't want to risk a secondary infection.'

'How bad is it?'

The hypnotic strokes slowed and then stopped. In a detached way, Matt realised the action of her hand seemed to be an answer in itself.

'Do I need to prepare Nicky?' he said. And Doreen. And himself.

'I won't lie to you, Matt. It's a very serious illness. The next twenty-four to forty-eight hours are critical. If we've caught it early enough, he might survive. I'd like to be more positive but at this stage his chances are about fifty-fifty.'

He swallowed. The feeling of helplessness returned in double measure. 'Is there anything I can do?'

She hesitated. 'Could you hold him while I put in the drip? It'll be a lot easier.'

He nodded then waited while Caitlin collected the instruments she needed from the tray. When she was ready, he gathered Spotty in a firm but gentle hold. The lack of resistance from the pup was sobering. No struggling at all, not even with the loud buzz of the clippers Caitlin used to shave the front of one thin foreleg.

'Could you hold his leg here, like this?' She demonstrated by wrapping her thumb and forefinger around Spotty's upper leg in a makeshift tourniquet. 'I'll get you to tighten in a moment.'

After tearing open a sterile pack, she swabbed the skin thoroughly with antiseptic.

'Okay, I'm ready.'

Matt tightened his grip. He watched Caitlin's long, slender fingers expertly slide a cannula into the vein. With it taped into position, she reached for the line from the waiting saline bag. Her eyes were intent as she took a few moments to check the drip rate.

Holding the pup's over-warm body, he watched Caitlin wrap

gauze around the leg with neat, efficient movements. The bright red crinkled bandage she finished off with looked inappropriately jolly against the stark white of the pup's coat.

She fastened a wide collar to his neck. 'Let's get him into the cage.'

Taking care not to touch the bandaged leg, Matt did as Caitlin asked, aware of her moving beside him with the saline bag in hand.

After she'd hung the bag above the cage, she closed the door and turned to face him.

'Try not to worry, Matt.' She reached out to touch his arm, her fingers light and warm against his skin. 'You got him here quickly. He's young and strong and the symptoms have only just appeared.'

'Thanks.'

With her eyes still on his, she smiled slightly, 'You know I'll do my best for him.'

'I know.'

When she removed her hand, he felt a disproportionate sense of loss.

After a small silence, he said, 'I should go.'

'You should.' She stepped out into the small hall and opened the back door.

'You'll ring if there are any problems?' He paused beside her.

'I will, yes.'

'I don't just mean with the pup.'

'That's kind of you. Doreen's made the same offer.'

'She's worried that you're staying at the clinic alone.' *So am I.* But he left the words unsaid.

'I know, yes. I'll be thoroughly spoiled by the time I leave.'

Matt felt his gut tighten. There she was again, bringing up the temporary nature of her stay. Was it to remind him or herself? Was she counting the days until she left Garrangay? He wasn't. Far from it. The more he saw of her the more he wanted her.

He stood there a moment longer, hands in his pockets. He

wanted to challenge her, point out the advantages of staying in Garrangay, of staying with him. But now was not the time. She had work to do and he needed to go home.

He leaned down, pressed his lips to her cheek. The delightful light perfume she wore filled his nostrils. Her sudden stillness, the startled look she flicked up as he drew back gave him some small satisfaction.

'Bye, Matt.' She stepped back, folding her arms. 'Give Doreen my best and tell her to take care of herself or I'll be around to growl. In fact, I'll be around to growl, anyway. Maybe tomorrow.'

'I'll pass on the message.' He smiled wryly. 'She might take more notice of you. She's adopted you into the family.'

An odd parade of expressions flitted across her mobile face. Joy, guilt. Despair?

'Caitlin?'

'I'd better get in and check on Spotty. Goodbye, Matt.'

She was right. They both had other priorities right now.

Gravel crunched beneath his feet as he crossed to his vehicle.

Like breaking the news to Nicky that his pup was fighting to survive?

And like Doreen. Her angina underlined the fragility of life.

A chill slithered down his spine. Change was coming and he couldn't stop it. He clenched his fingers around the steering wheel. He'd do everything he could to protect his little family but it might not be enough.

With one last look at the clinic, he pulled out of the driveway and headed for home.

CHAPTER FOURTEEN

'HELLO, SWEETIE.' Caitlin stifled a yawn as she peered at the drip chamber of the pup's intravenous line. Still running well and the bag didn't need changing yet.

She glanced at the clock on the wall. Not quite two in the morning. Nearly seven hours since Matt had brought him in.

Crouching to look in to the cage, her nose wrinkled.

'Phew, puppy. That's bad.'

Spotty's soft brown eyes blinked up at her glumly. He didn't make any effort to raise his head.

After snapping on a pair of gloves, she unlatched the cage and began changing the soiled paper on the floor.

By the time she'd resettled the dog and cleaned up, she was wide awake. She walked through the clinic towards the kitchen thinking she'd make a hot drink to take back to bed.

A strong beam of light shone through the window behind her, swinging brightly across the wall.

An emergency? No one had called. She changed direction, grabbing a white coat and thrusting her arms into the sleeves. Her fingers were still busy with the buttons as she turned to the door. Through the glass panel she could see a familiar figure.

Matt!

She pulled open the door.

The steady whirring pop of frog song resonated in the

distance as she stared at him. Her eyes roved his face, taking in his grave expression. The porch light glistened on his full bottom lip as though he'd just run his tongue across the surface.

And then her mind unfroze. Panic had her reaching out blindly to clutch the door frame. 'Oh, God! Doreen. Is she—?'

'She's fine.'

Caitlin's knees turned to jelly as the blood seemed to seep away from her brain.

'Caitlin! Doreen's fine.' Matt's voice was sharp, but she still couldn't seem to process the words.

She heard him swear softly and was vaguely aware of him stepping close, gathering her against his hard body, moving her back into the clinic.

'I'm okay.' Her voice sounded far away, almost dreamy. 'You gave me a fright. That's all. When I saw you…'

'You thought the worst.'

'Yes.' Something pressed into the back of her knees.

'I'm going to sit you down, sweetheart.' Her body was gently folded into a chair and her head pressed down between her knees.

'I'm okay. Really.' Her slippered feet came back into clear focus as blood rushed back to her head. Now that she understood she wasn't in imminent danger of losing her aunt, her system began to react to Matt's nearness.

'Of course you are.' Fingers stroked the sensitive nape of her neck in a soothing motion. Her skin quivered with delight under the tiny caress.

When he lifted her wrist, she realised he was going to take her pulse. No way did she want him feeling her heartbeat's frantic bumping and surging.

More insistent against his restraining hand now, she pushed herself upright in the chair. Since he was crouched beside her, his face was close. Green eyes searched hers with clinical thoroughness.

'So, if Doreen's all right, what are you doing here?' she croaked.

He looked faintly sheepish. The weight of his hand slipped from her shoulder. 'I'm on my way home from a callout. I saw your light on so I thought I'd check everything was okay.'

'It is, yes,' she said faintly.

'Good.' His eyes warmed, roaming her features, settling on her lips. Heat climbed into her cheeks.

She looked away and for the first time realised that he'd walked her through to Bob's office. The room seemed impossibly small with him in it. Panic cramped her chest. She had to get out.

'Why don't you come and see Spotty while you're here?' She got to her feet, relieved when there was no sign of residual weakness in her legs. 'I've just checked him. He's holding his own.'

She led the way back to the isolation area where she handed Matt an apron and overshoes. 'Here, you'll need these.'

Concentrating on her patient helped blunt the effect of his disturbing presence.

Spotty eyed them forlornly, his head resting awkwardly on the wide collar between his front paws, as Caitlin unlatched the cage.

Matt crouched beside her, reaching in to fondle the floppy ears.

She watched his hands so gentle on the pup's head. Spotty's eyes slowly closed on a sigh under the steady caress. Caitlin shifted her gaze to Matt's profile, unable to resist the opportunity to devour tiny details. The faint stubble on his cheek, his ear tucked so neatly against his head, the firm line of his jaw. The cables of his hand-knitted jumper stretched across broad shoulders, the way the blunt-cut edge of his hair curved into his neck. A couple of sections of the hair were slightly out of place, perhaps ruffled as he'd pulled on the apron. She stifled the urge to reach out and smooth them down.

'He looks miserable.' A muscle twitched along his jaw.

Dragging her wayward mind back to business, Caitlin focussed on the pup. 'He does.'

'How is he?'

'He's stable, Matt, and that's a good thing. I wish I could say more than that but I can't. Maybe later today.'

Keep thinking of the basics. He'll be on his way home in a few minutes. Last night, when he'd brought Spotty into the clinic, had been so easy. Matt had been a client with a patient. She'd had something to do, been able to take refuge behind her job.

'I know.' His eyes were sombre when they met hers. 'You said twenty-four hours. I'm sorry. I didn't mean to push. I wanted to be able to give Nicky and Doreen good news in the morning.'

His obvious concern for his mother and his son melted her heart, made her want to offer him comfort.

'I'm—I was about to make a hot chocolate. Only one of the packet varieties, but you'd be welcome to...' She trailed off. Damn. Was she insane? Hadn't she just been counting the minutes until he left? Now here she was inviting this disturbing man to stay longer. Before he could answer, she said, 'Though no doubt you want get home to your bed.'

Even worse. She bit her lip.

'Hot chocolate sounds good,' he said. 'Thanks.'

'We can wash up outside.' She stood up, aware that Matt was following her lead.

She dried her hands and watched Matt soaping his. He had strong and broad palms with long, well-shaped fingers. They were hands that promised strength and reliability, hands to hold and comfort. Hands to caress...

She shoved the towel back on to the rail. 'I'll put the kettle on. Come through when you're done.'

In the kitchen, she stood staring into the free-standing cabinet serving temporary duty as a pantry, her chilled palms cupping her cheeks. At this indecent hour of the night, her biorhythms must be incredibly low. That's why she was noticing things, feeling things she didn't want to. Hadn't she told him they couldn't be involved? She didn't belong here. But all her denials would count for nothing if she couldn't keep herself under control.

'Caitlin?'

'Matt.' Her hand shot out to grab the packet, fumbling then managing to catch it as it tipped off the shelf. 'Um, have a seat.'

Think of a nice safe subject, she commanded herself mentally as he hitched a hip onto one of the bar stools at the short length of usable bench. After flicking the switch on the jug, she collected two large mugs. 'Have you had any answers to your lost-dog notices, then?'

'Nothing yet.'

'It's early days but I suspect you might have a dog if you want one.' She spooned a generous serving of the drink powder into each mug. 'Perhaps even if you don't want one.'

His answering grin was wry. 'Nicky will be over the moon.'

'You won't be so pleased?'

He ran a hand around the back of his neck. 'I've been expecting someone to answer the advertisements.'

'The next logical step would be a home-wanted notice. You're welcome to put one up here.'

'Are you kidding?' He chuckled softly. 'Lost-dog notices are one thing, *home-wanted* signs and my life wouldn't be worth living. He's wormed his way into everyone's heart.' After a tiny beat, he added, 'Including mine.'

The jug clicked off and Caitlin picked it up. The rich aroma of chocolate wafted up as she poured hot water over the powder. She pushed a mug across to him before sliding onto a stool opposite.

'Thanks.' His eyes flicked around the room as he blew on the edge of the drink before taking a cautious sip. 'How are you coping with Bob's renovations?'

'I've been in worse.' Relaxed, with him safely on the other side of the bench, Caitlin looked around the room at the cobweb-covered wooden frame, the exposed wires and plumbing.

'At least I don't have to carry my own water here. I don't think I stood in a normal domestic kitchen until I went to boarding school.'

'Mum's worried you'll starve.'

'She's a darling.' She grinned at him. 'Though she shouldn't be fussing over me.'

'Try stopping her.'

'Her angina,' began Caitlin tentatively. 'How—how serious is it?' She really wanted to ask if a shock would be too much, if it could precipitate a heart attack. She wanted to be told that it wouldn't.

'It's been stable with medication. And she goes into Hamilton for regular check-ups.' He smiled wryly. 'It's pointless telling her to slow down. Though I've tried. Thankfully, she does pace herself a bit better these days.'

Not quite the definitive reassurance that she was after. 'You'd like her to slow down more?'

'Yes. And no. She puts me to shame.'

'In what way?'

'She seizes life and marches right along with it.'

Caitlin turned over his words as she swallowed the last of her chocolate drink. A thin layer of foam coated the base of the pottery. 'And you think you don't?'

'I march…cautiously.'

She laughed. 'Marching is marching, surely. And you have responsibilities.'

'Yes, I do. And I tell myself that. But I sometimes wonder if it's a handy excuse, too.' He propped his elbows on the bench and leaned forward. With his eyes heavy lidded and focussed on her mouth, the relaxed atmosphere changed abruptly. 'It'd be nice to do something incautious every now and then. Don't you think?' His voice was low and inviting.

'I'm not sure.' It was all she could do not to stutter.

'For instance, if I was less cautious I would offer to help you clean up that chocolate on your top lip.'

She put her hand up, shielding her mouth as she licked her lip.

'No,' he said softly when she took her hand away. 'Still there. Let me help.'

Suddenly he was a lot closer. Her heart stopped on a hard beat then jolted into a frantic gallop as Matt leaned over the bench, his intent obvious. She could have pulled back, out of reach. It would have been so simple. Instead, she watched him moving nearer, watched his gaze roam her face, resettle on her lips. She longed to moisten them, make them ready for his kiss, for that was surely what he was going to do. She could feel his breath on her skin, a soft caress, as he angled his head. Her eyelids wanted to flutter closed—she forced them open, met his eyes, saw the glitter of his hunger, his need.

His kiss was the barest touch, light, questioning. The warm, dry pressure of his mouth, the moist stroke of his tongue, the tug as he bit down gently on her bottom lip for a moment. She shut her eyes, giving her senses up to the moment. Only their lips were touching but she could feel the response through her entire body, a growing, glowing warmth.

'Caitlin?'

'Mmm?' she managed as she opened her eyes. The gravelly rasp of the sound was a surprise.

'Come out to dinner with me on Saturday night. Just the two of us.' He'd withdrawn a minute distance, only needing to tilt forward slightly for his mouth to cover hers again.

'Dinner?'

'Yeah. You know—the two of us with a knife and fork each and food. A date.'

Caitlin felt her mind clearing, her natural caution swinging back into place.

'Ah, one of those. I've heard of them.'

'I'm sensing a "but" here.'

She reached out to grasp her empty mug, circling the bottom on the bench as she considered her answer.

A grin lit up his face briefly. 'You don't find me attractive?

I'm polite, presentable, reasonably well behaved. Good sense of humour, non-smoker, social drinker.'

A snort of laughter escaped before she could suppress it. 'You sound like an advertisement for the "companion wanted" column.'

'Steady job, hard worker, low maintenance, low risk, house trained. Good teeth, strong bones, straight legs.' He grinned.

'Hmm. Or perhaps a breeding programme,' she said.

He sent her a wicked look. 'Proven fatherhood material.'

She swallowed. 'Tsk. I left myself wide open for that one, didn't I? Still, you could have resisted.'

'Sorry.' But he didn't look at all repentant. He removed the mug she fidgeted with, setting it aside so he could take her hands. 'There's a spark between us. You can't deny it, Caitlin. We've both fought it for our different reasons. But why shouldn't we explore where it takes us?'

Because she'd already had a taste of how powerfully he affected her. Any more and she could be a blithering, submissive mess. She didn't want to lose herself, become invisible. The way her father had disappeared in her parents' marriage.

'There are lots of reasons.' She watched his thumbs rub across her knuckles, soaking in the comforting sensation while she tried to remember what those reasons were. Thankfully her tired brain latched onto something that was safe to say. 'You've other people to consider. Your son, your mother.'

'Both of whom adore you.'

Her heart basked in happiness for a tiny moment before she forced herself to face reality. She was bringing them bad news, would cause them pain, especially Doreen. 'I'll leave in a few weeks. Why risk hurting each other?'

'We might not hurt each other. We might discover we're meant for each other and you won't be able to tear yourself away from me.'

'Perhaps that's what I'm really afraid of.' She blinked, mentally reeling from leaving herself so exposed, so open.

He groaned. 'You can't say something like that and not expect me to follow through on it.'

'Matt—'

'Hush, Caitlin.' He reached out to touch his fingers briefly to her lips, stopping her protest. His hand slipped around to the back of her neck, tilting her face back up to his. 'I think we communicate much better like this.'

'Far too well, I'd say,' she murmured breathlessly, when his lips released hers.

'All I'm asking for…' his mouth moved over hers again '…is one little dinner date.'

Could she? Did she dare? She couldn't think properly with his teeth gently sinking into her lower lip. 'Okay.'

'Good.' He ran a light finger over her mouth. 'Thanks for the chocolate. All of it.' His mouth curved into a smile as he stood. 'Go to bed. I'll lock the door on my way out. Sleep well, sweet Caitlin.'

When he was gone, she rested her chin in her hands and contemplated their empty mugs. Had she just made a huge mistake?

She didn't feel any closer to talking to Doreen. A couple of times she'd tried but there had always been an interruption or a concern for her aunt's health. And the truth was she'd welcomed the opportunity to put it off each time. Revealing the news about her father was going to be a shock. And she was a coward, afraid of hurting the people she wanted to be close to. Afraid that whatever wedge had driven Martin away would work to push her out, too. But if she didn't take a chance, she would never know.

She needed to be braver. And perhaps, if she was careful, if she could find the right time, the right words, she could be worthy of Doreen's love, a relationship with Matt. A future in Garrangay.

If she could do this right, maybe they would want her to stay, even after she'd told them the truth.

Matt padded along the hallway in his socks, pausing to push open Nicky's door. Soft light from the hall lamp spilled across the pillow and a thatch of tussled dark brown hair. The colour was part of his ex-wife's legacy to their son.

The rest of the bed was a jumbled mound. Spiderman was caught in mid-leap on the quilt cover and clung precariously to the edge of the bed.

He crossed the room and bent to straighten the bedding as much as possible without disturbing Nicky. He needn't have worried. His son slept with a soundness that implied absolute confidence in his world. Matt wondered if his sleep had been the same at that age.

He brushed the silky-fine fringe from his son's forehead. Caitlin was right. There were other people he needed to consider. But there was no reason why he couldn't begin paving the way. And he didn't anticipate any problems with either Doreen or Nicky.

With one last look at his sleeping child, he closed the door and continued down the hall to his own room.

His son's capacity for trust amazed Matt. He'd explained about Spotty's illness, doing his best to prepare his son for a bad outcome. But Nicky had been utterly convinced that Caitlin wouldn't let the pup die. That faith was at once touching and terrifying.

Even Doreen, who should know better, was confident that all would be well now the dog was in Caitlin's hands. Poor Caitlin. She had a lot to live up to with those two putting her on a pedestal.

Matt didn't want her on a pedestal. He wanted her as part of his life, part of his family. And he wanted her in his bed.

He stripped off and slid between cool sheets. Was Caitlin doing the same down the road? He tortured himself with the image for a long minute. Sleep suddenly seemed a long way off. Hands clasped behind his head, he lay staring at the ceiling, tracing the shadowed relief of the plaster rose.

Caitlin would never know what it had cost him to leave her tonight. Had it been just half an hour ago? Instinct had warned him not to push, regardless of how much he wanted to. Why did he have the feeling he worked against time? Urgency and caution, an impossible combination to balance. Did he deserve accolades for his sensitivity or ridicule for being a faint-hearted fool?

He rolled over to thump the pillow into a more comfortable shape. His kiss had put colour into her cheeks, a dreamy glow into her beautiful grey eyes.

Saturday night was too far away. Thirty-six hours. Perhaps he could drop by again to check Spotty's progress. He grimaced.

No doubt about it—he was a goner.

Now, if only Caitlin was as far gone, everything would be perfect.

CHAPTER FIFTEEN

'TIME we weren't here, Nicky,' said Matt, checking his watch. 'Clean your teeth and grab your gear.'

''Kay, Dad.' Nicky jammed the last of his toast in his mouth.

'Don't forget your lunch.' Doreen held out the box that she'd just packed.

Nicky pivoted at the door and raced back to the bench. 'Thanks, Nanna,' he mumbled around the mouthful of food.

Matt listened to his son's footsteps pounding down the hall, could picture the moment he hit the top of the staircase by the change in tempo.

Instead of making a move to follow, Matt watched Doreen come back to the table and begin tidying. He watched her hands as she closed the top of the cereal packet, screwed the lid back onto the strawberry-jam jar, wiped up a small pool of spilled milk. His fingers drummed lightly on the table. This was a good opportunity to speak to her. Alone. Now.

'I've got a date with Caitlin on Saturday night.' *Damn. That had come out so baldly.* Where was the carefully worded spiel he'd worked on in the shower fifteen minutes ago? 'Tomorrow.'

Doreen looked up from the plates she'd stacked, her eyes wide and her mouth dropping open in a stunned expression. 'Oh, my.'

He narrowed his eyes at the unexpected negative response. 'What? What's wrong?' he said warily.

'You're…just so…smitten.'

To Matt's sensitive ears it seemed like an accusation.

'I *like* her. A lot. Yes. What's wrong with that?'

Double damn. What was wrong with *him*? He sounded like a schoolboy defending his latest crush. In an effort to cover his agitation, he picked up the coffee-pot and tilted it over his mug. Black liquid splashed up over the edge and puddled on the table.

'There's nothing wrong with it. Nothing at all. Not a thing.' Doreen leaned forward and whisked the dishcloth under his mug before he could fix it himself.

Matt stifled a sigh and reached for his drink to take a deep fortifying swig. The fresh brew scalded the roof of his mouth. He swallowed quickly and felt the super-hot liquid travel down every inch.

'I thought you liked her,' he said, wondering why he'd imagined this might be simple.

'Oh, yes, I do. I do. Very much.' Doreen carried the dishes to the sink and busied her hands with gloves and sponges and detergent.

Matt had the distinct impression she was avoiding looking at him. 'So, what's the problem? Last week, you were match-making.'

'Yes, and I do want…. But that was before I was sure—' She stopped abruptly.

'Before you were sure about what?'

Clattering dishes and running water were the only sounds in the kitchen for a long moment. Finally, Doreen turned away from the bench, soapsuds dripping from her rubber gloves and a worried look on her face.

'Before she took the locum. She'll be leaving in a few weeks.'

'I'm taking her out for dinner, Mum, not proposing.' *Marvellous! Where had* that *little gem come from? Another Freudian slip?*

'Yes, dear, I know. It's…I—I don't want to see you get

hurt.' She turned back to the sink but Matt had the feeling she hadn't finished speaking yet. 'Caitlin's only going to be here for such a short time. Only until Gary's better. Then Bob will be back.'

Her comments tallied so completely with his own misgivings and with Caitlin's comments that he had to suppress a grimace.

'But she *might* stay longer, mightn't she? Why wouldn't she want to?' He sipped cautiously at his coffee. The liquid tasted bitter on his tongue. Crossing to the bench to tip it out, he continued, 'I've got so much to offer. Needy single father, country bumpkin, job with long hours so I'll hardly get underfoot.' He twisted his lips into a smile. 'Hell, Mum, I'm quite a catch.'

'Matthew!' Doreen looked up at him, her smoky blue-grey eyes full of reproach.

'I'm sorry, Mum.' He sighed and ran a hand around the back of his neck. 'I know you're concerned for me. When it comes to Caitlin, I'm concerned for me too. But I'll have to take my chances. And I've put the pieces back together before, haven't I?'

'Yes, you have.' She looked at him shrewdly. 'But I'm not sure it's the same. If it had been, I wonder whether you'd have left the city, come back to Garrangay.'

The piercing insight into his marriage left him momentarily speechless.

'I know there's chemistry between you and Caitlin. I've felt it myself,' said Doreen, sounding resigned. When he continued to stare at her, she smiled at him. 'And don't mock yourself, Matthew Gardiner. You are a *great* catch for some lucky woman. I should know—I brought you up to be one.'

'Perhaps you can put in a good word for me,' he said wryly.

'Perhaps.'

'Mum—'

'I know, dear. You're only joking. So am I. I wouldn't interfere.'

'Unless it suits you,' he said with a grin, as footsteps thundered back towards them.

Nicky exploded back into the kitchen, thrusting his arms into the straps of his bag. 'I'm ready.'

'Got everything? Lunch, homework?'

'Yep. Bye, Nanna.' Nicky crossed to his grandmother for his kiss goodbye.

'Let's go.' Matt dropped a kiss on Doreen's forehead. 'Don't worry, Mum, it'll work out. See you later.'

He followed his son out to the car, mentally girding himself to break the news about his date. Surely it couldn't be worse than the scene with Doreen…could it?

Saturday night and she had a date. She hadn't been this giddy about a date since…. Ever.

Caitlin smoothed a tiny amount of blusher over her cheekbones. Her reflection told her it was hardly necessary. Anticipation made her eyes sparkle, her skin glow.

Not even having to borrow clothes from Haley for the evening could dampen her spirits. Funny how things had a way of happening when a person was least prepared.

Getting invited out to dinner…

Learning about a long-lost aunt…

Finding a man who would be so easy to love.

Not that she was *in love*. With her hand pressed flat on her sternum, she could feel the wild skitter of her heart. Life was getting very complicated.

She picked up the slinky gold top she'd laid out on the bed earlier and slipped it over her head. The fabric felt cool and light and moved in a way that clung to her breasts and the curve of her waist. It made her feel…sexy, which was probably *not* a good thing at all. How could she keep Matt in line when she felt poised to leap off a precipice herself?

No amount of common sense stopped her bubbling excitement. Not even reminding herself that she had real reasons to be cautious.

Tomorrow she would do something about one of those reasons, she would try to talk to her aunt. But tonight...she wanted tonight for herself.

She slipped her feet into the strappy sandals that matched the top. More of Haley's generosity. She'd been *handled* by Bob's veterinary nurse, no two ways about it.

She was still astounded about their conversation over yesterday afternoon's surgery. All she'd done had been to ask a simple question as she'd closed up a feline abdomen. She grinned wryly as she remembered.

'Is there somewhere handy to buy a nice evening top, Haley? In Hamilton, perhaps? I don't want anything too fancy.'

Her assistant had looked up from the anaesthetic equipment, delight shining in her eyes above the green mask. 'Oh, wow! Matt's asked you out, hasn't he?'

'Wh-what makes you think that?' Just as well she hadn't been in the middle of a delicate surgical procedure. Her fingers had turned to thumbs.

'Gosh, Caitlin. Everyone knows he's got the—ah, that he's, um, sweet on you.'

So much for discretion. It sounded as though she and Matt were a hot topic in the town. Very hot. The thought was unnerving.

How would Matt feel about the gossip? Did he know? And had Doreen and Nicky heard it?

How did they feel about Matt taking her out? He would have given them some explanation about what he was doing this evening. Did Nicky mind? Or did he feel threatened by the idea of his father taking a woman out on a date?

It sounded like Sophie played a very small role in her son's life. But even in situations like that children often harboured secret hopes that their parents would get back together.

Or maybe the date had Nicky and Doreen's blessing. Caitlin

smoothed her hand over her stomach, wishing she could calm the nerves bouncing there. According to Matt, his mother and his son adored her. But, then, none of them knew her, *really* knew her. Would they feel the same way if they did? If they realised how closed in she felt sometimes, how desperately inadequate and lonely.

'You look gorgeous.'

Matt's wide, appreciative smile—now, *that* was gorgeous, thought Caitlin, her heart jittering. She didn't even try to suppress her answering grin.

'Thank you. So do you.' And he did. Smartly dressed in dark grey trousers with a burgundy shirt and a tie with interlinked patterns in shades of both colours. And he was here to take her out. 'Mine's borrowed plumage. Holiday packing doesn't extend to evening wear.'

'Haley?'

'It was, yes.' She debated for a moment whether to tell him that Haley had guessed why the clothes were needed.

Before she could make up her mind, he reached out and took her hand. 'Hey, thanks for ringing about Spotty this morning.' His voice was soft and mellow, filled with caring warmth, as though she'd done something really special.

'Oh, um, I knew you'd all want to know that our star patient had turned the corner.' She squeezed his fingers quickly before claiming her hand back to rummage for her keys.

'We appreciated it. I appreciated it.'

She swallowed and clasped the keys firmly in front of her. 'I—I wanted to say something last night when you rang but it was still too soon. I'm confident he'll make a full recovery now.'

'Thanks.'

She stepped outside, locking the door behind her. As soon as she began walking beside him, Matt put his hand in the small of her back to usher her towards the car. The divine fabric pressed hot and silky onto her skin where he touched.

'I'm afraid Haley guessed why I needed something to go out in,' she said, filling the small silence, hoping to take her mind off the exquisite sensations spreading out from her lumbar region. 'If you had any hopes of keeping things quiet…'

'No hopes at all. The residents of Garrangay knew I was interested in you almost before I did.'

'I guess it's one of the hazards of living in a small community?' she said slowly. He seemed very philosophical but she couldn't help feeling dismayed about being the topic of gossip. Was it guilt at her deception that made it seem so subtly threatening?

'Yes.' He removed his hand to open the car door.

'Thanks.' She lowered herself into the seat, still bemused by regret and relief in equal measure. The imprint of his fingers lingered on her skin. His touch was powerful beyond anything reasonable.

She watched him walk around the front of the car and slide in behind the steering-wheel. He started the engine then twisted to face her, laying his hand across the back of her seat as he looked over his shoulder, out the rear window.

His closeness was at once disconcerting and exciting. Thank goodness his attention was entirely on reversing out of the parking spot. His subtle musky aftershave enveloped her senses, making her want to lean forward and breathe deeply until the fragrance of him filled her completely. To burrow into the crook of his neck where the column of his throat met with the dark shirt collar.

Her eyes traced the line of his jaw—smooth shaven and slightly shiny. A neat ear, detached lobes—perfect to nibble on.

Heavens, she had to get a grip. She'd be throwing herself at him in a minute.

She swallowed, dragging her gaze away from his face along a nicely muscled arm tapering to a strong wrist. Her gaze settled on the hand manoeuvring the steering-wheel. He had great hands, long lean fingers. Practical and sensitive. She hadn't been a person to notice hands—but that had changed since meeting Matt. And when he touched her...

No, don't think about that now.

Find something to talk about. What had they been discussing? *Oh, yes, small towns.*

He braked and began to swivel back towards the front.

'Don't you mind everyone knowing your business?'

He paused, half turned, and focussed on her. 'Does it worry you?'

'Not worry exactly. But neither am I thrilled about it.'

He slotted the gear lever into drive and they moved smoothly out of the parking area.

'I grew up in the foster-system,' he said, after a long moment. 'All sorts of people knew my business. Social workers, police, teachers, doctors. Everyone in Garrangay.'

Guilt stabbed at her. Worrying about an evening out being common knowledge was so petty compared to Matt's life under the community's spotlight. 'I'm sorry, Matt, that was insensitive of me.'

'It was a long time ago, Caitlin.'

'Did you...did you want leave it behind sometimes? Be anonymous?'

'I did leave it behind while I was studying and first married. But the bottom line is I like the town and the people.'

Matt gathered his thoughts in silence. A lot hinged on Caitlin understanding his attachment to Garrangay, why he'd come back, why he stayed.

And why he wouldn't want to leave.

If they had a relationship, she'd need to stay. He couldn't move back to Melbourne. Not now. Maybe he wasn't being fair, but too many people relied on him.

He chose his words with care.

'My mother was born in Garrangay and lived most of her life here. This is where she came when she was pregnant.

People did what they could for her and for me. And I had Doreen and Pete.'

'Yes, of course.'

'The interest is well meant. Well, most of it.' He grinned as he glanced over at her. Solemn grey eyes met his and held for a moment. He stifled a small sigh. 'A bit overwhelming if you're not used to it.'

His tension level cranked a little higher as he waited for her reply.

'I suppose I *am* used to it, growing up around my mother's research projects,' she said slowly, as though making a discovery. 'Perhaps it's being in someone else's fishbowl that makes it unnerving.'

Her hands lay on top of her small evening bag in her lap. He reached over and gave her fingers a quick squeeze.

'Well, we've escaped from the bowl tonight. Let's make the most of it,' he said, hoping to lighten the mood.

'Deal.' She sent him a mischievous smile. 'As long as you remember I'll be throwing you back early if you misbehave.'

'Best behaviour. Absolutely. I won't do anything without your approval.'

'I'm not sure I'm greatly reassured,' she said dryly. 'And that would be a reflection on my character, not yours.'

Matt laughed, appreciating her quirky honesty. His system kicked with the confirmation that the attraction wasn't all on his side. It was tempting to throw caution aside, to let the heat burn between them as brightly as it could. But caution and patience had brought them this far. He could keep to his plan...which was not to say that he might not rupture something with all this self-control.

'This is grand,' said Caitlin, looking around after they'd been seated with menus. They were near a cosy bay-window recess.

'Yes. And unexpected after seeing the exterior.' Matt smiled ruefully. 'I wondered what we were in for.'

'It looked a bit dire, didn't it?'

The shabby exterior of the old two-storey hotel, clad in metal scaffolding, had given no hint of the wonderful atmosphere inside. A gleaming blackwood bar stretched along one wall, oiled wood dado panelling, cream walls. Subdued lighting from coach lamps and candles on the tables gave an aura of stepping back in time.

Flames leapt and flickered behind the glass panel of a wood heater at one end of the room, countering the chill of the night.

'Nicky never doubted you'd pull Spotty through,' said Matt, breaking the small silence after the waiter had taken their order. 'Neither did Doreen.'

'I'm glad Spotty and I didn't let them down.' Caitlin fidgeted with the end of her knife for a moment. 'It's a big responsibility, isn't it? When people believe in you like that?'

Matt's smile made her toes curl. 'I know. You don't want to let them down.'

'Yes. I hate disappointing people.' The memory of her ongoing deception tightened her throat. 'It—it's hard to avoid sometimes.'

'I believed in you, too.' He leaned forward, his eyes holding hers.

'Mmm.' An odd claustrophobic feeling swept over her and she glanced away, struggling to think of something to lighten the moment. 'But I imagine your belief came with a healthy dose of acceptance that bad things can happen no matter how hard a person might try to make it otherwise.'

'True.' Matt smiled.

She relaxed. 'Dalmatians need a lot of exercise. They were carriage dogs in England, you know. Perhaps even chariot dogs in ancient Egypt. Spotty comes from a long line of energetic ancestors.'

'But if he's a pedigree, doesn't it make it unlikely that he'd be dumped?'

'If he was show-dog or breeding material, it would. But he

has a lot of brown marking with the black. Tricolouration is considered a defect.'

'I don't think Nicky minds what colour his spots are as long as we keep him.' He looked so pleased about the idea that Caitlin hoped no one came forward to make a claim.

Spotty was part of Matt's family, a part of Doreen's family. Caitlin felt a small rush of envy. Animals didn't doubt their right to belong. If only it was that easy for people. But, then, animals didn't keep secrets from loved ones either.

A second waiter arrived with the wine and, after pouring some into their glasses, nestled the bottle into an ice bucket.

'A toast,' said Matt, his green gaze holding hers as he raised his glass. 'To itinerant veterinarians.'

Caitlin reached for her glass and chinked it lightly against the edge of his then sipped the chilled fruity wine.

'I'm glad you're here.' The dark warm glow deep in his eyes sent shivers through her system.

'Thank you. So am I.'

'I'm especially glad you're here tonight. With me.' His voice caressed sensitive nerve endings. Her heart thumped wildly, the force of it pulsing through her body. He made her feel so special and for tonight she wanted to bask in that warmth.

By the end of the meal Caitlin knew she'd fallen even deeper under Matt's spell.

There was a lull in their conversation after the waiter took away their plates but it wasn't uncomfortable. Caitlin reached out to toy with the base of her wineglass.

Matt's hand covered hers and she watched his fingers play with the plain gold band on her middle finger. The smooth pads ran lightly over her knuckles and every nerve in her body seemed to centre on the sensitive skin that he was touching.

'Did you wear a wedding ring when you were married?' Appalled at her gaffe, Caitlin stared at him. The question had burst out without conscious thought. 'Oh, dear. Don't answer that. I don't know what made me ask such a thing.'

'That's all right.' He smiled slightly. 'Yes, I did wear a ring.'

She glanced down at the fingers of his left hand where they rested over hers. 'You've no mark to show.'

'It's been a long time since I took it off.' His eyes were solemn, steady. 'Does it bother you that I've been married? That I'm divorced?'

'No. Why would it?'

He shrugged. 'Divorce means a marriage that failed.'

'Perhaps staying together when things are bad is a failure.' Though she couldn't imagine living with Matt would be a hardship. The people around him were so secure, confident of their place in his life. He was a man to rely on.

'Perhaps. Sophie and I had no idea of what to expect from marriage or from each other.'

'Don't you learn as you go along?'

'Sure. But better to start with some idea. To have kids, not to have kids. How it's going to work if you do.' His gaze dropped back to her hand. 'After Nicky was born, I expected us to work out times so we could share looking after him. Less time in day care, you know. But Sophie wouldn't slow down. I hated the thought of bringing him up in the city as a latch-key kid. We made a mistake with our marriage but I didn't want our son to be the one to pay for it.'

'It must have been difficult,' said Caitlin.

'Not for Sophie. She didn't want the responsibility of being a mother so she avoided it by working longer and longer hours.' He released her hand, reaching for his glass. Caitlin watched his throat move as he swallowed. He stared into the pale gold liquid for a long moment. 'And after a while she didn't want the responsibility of being a wife either.'

There was a small pause, his fingers whitened on the glass and then he said, 'She avoided that by having an affair.'

'Oh, Matt.' Caitlin's heart went out to him as she absorbed the shock of his revelation.

His eyes flicked back to hers, intense, sharply focussed. 'What do you expect from marriage, Caitlin?'

'I—I'm not sure.' He was so brave, so devastatingly honest that she felt compelled to try to be the same. As far as she could. 'I don't want what my parents had. An unequal marriage.'

'Because your father wasn't academic?'

'No, not because of that.' She pursed her lips for a moment. 'Perhaps one-sided is closer to what I mean. He was there for my mother but the commitment wasn't returned.'

She withdrew her hand from his and twisted the gold band on her finger. 'This is my father's wedding ring.'

There was a small silence.

'He wanted you to have it?'

'No. He—he wants my mother to have it. I haven't had a chance to give it to her because I haven't seen her yet. She hasn't been able to make a time for us to meet.' The tinge of bitterness in her voice surprised her. She'd thought she'd got over the hurt that had caused. 'It's been a year since he passed away.'

'She wasn't with you when he died?'

'No. She didn't come back at all.' She shrugged. 'In some ways I was glad. My father and I became very close. He had a marvellous way of looking at the world that I miss very much.'

Caitlin frowned. This compulsion to confide in Matt was perplexing…and fraught with pitfalls. But some part of her seemed to be determined to do it. Perhaps because anything less than truth would be shabby in the face of his willingness to share his past. And she could tell him this much. Doreen had the right to know the rest of Martin's story first. And soon. Tomorrow, she promised herself.

'You looked after him while he was ill?'

'Yes and no. He stayed with me and mostly looked after both of us.' She rubbed the ring lightly. 'He spoiled me.'

'You deserved it.'

'Maybe, maybe not.' She gave him a small smile and changed the subject. To her relief, the conversation moved easily onto less sensitive ground. As they got up to leave an hour later Caitlin was struck by an unsettling feeling that Matt had allowed her to make the change.

Back at the clinic, Matt walked her to the door.

'I've had a lovely evening, Matt. Thank you for asking me out.'

'Thank *you*. I've enjoyed it, too.'

Caitlin paused on the first step and turned to face him. 'I'd ask you in for coffee but…'

'It wouldn't be a good idea.' He reached up to tuck her hair behind her ear. The light brush of his fingers made her knees tremble. 'I'd probably try to stay longer than I should.'

'I'd probably want to let you and it's too…'

'Soon? Tempting?'

'All of that. And complicated.'

He stepped forward, touching his lips to hers. She sank into his kiss, the familiarity and delight. Her eyes closed as she revelled in the thrill of holding him close.

She felt the huge shuddering breath he drew in as the warm anchor of his mouth lifted from hers. The expansion and contraction of his chest against hers as though he'd been running hard.

'Very complicated.'

Her eyelids opened reluctantly. 'Yes.'

'I should say goodbye.'

'You should, yes.'

Caitlin wondered if her legs would hold her up if he let her go too quickly. Her hands lingered on his shoulders as she searched for the will to move away. She had to be sensible and let him go. It *was* complicated and for more reasons than Matt realised. He thought her reluctance stemmed from her temporary status in Garrangay, but that was almost beginning to feel like a minor problem to Caitlin. She loved the rural town, the countryside, the people.

'The boys are playing cricket in Hamilton tomorrow morning. Would you like to go?'

She hesitated. Tomorrow she'd promised herself she'd speak to Doreen. Her father's ghost loomed large in her mind. It was past time to reveal his part in her arrival in Garrangay.

'Nicky would love to show off his bowling skills.'

'Now I think you're playing dirty.' She laughed softly. How could she resist the man and his son? Maybe she could go to the game and find time to speak to Doreen later in the day. 'I'd love to see Nicky's prowess.'

'I'll pick you up around nine.'

She watched him drive out of the car park, a grin on her lips. Cricket. She was going to a cricket game. Voluntarily. Her father would never have believed it. But, then, watching the game wasn't the main attraction, was it?

CHAPTER SIXTEEN

'OH. OH.'

The small distressed gasps sent warning prickles down Matt's neck.

'Mum?' He dropped Nicky's cricket gear and dashed back to the kitchen.

His mother was slowly subsiding into a chair at the table, a fist clenched in the centre of her chest, her face pale and drawn.

'What's wrong?' He crossed to her side, aware of Nicky following in his wake. A fine sheen of perspiration dampened her skin.

'Oh, dear.' Her voice shook. 'Awful…heartburn.'

'Tell me where the pain is.' Was it an MI? God, he couldn't lose her. He ruthlessly suppressed his fear. Any sign of panic from him would be disastrous for his mother, for Nicky.

'In my chest and throat.' Her clenched hand rubbed along her sternum as though the pain could be erased through bone and flesh.

He laid a hand on her shoulder, feeling anxiety cramp his own chest. 'Just started?' A quick glance at his watch. Eight-thirty.

'I had a bit when I first got up. Nothing like this.'

'Did you take any angina medication then?' He breathed deeply, forcing his voice to stay calm.

'Yes. Antacids as well. It stopped straight away.' Her pain-filled eyes lifted to his in a silent plea.

'Good.' He gave her shoulder a quick squeeze of reassurance. 'Your tabs in the medicine cabinet?'

Her gaze went to the small cabinet at the end of the kitchen. 'Yes.'

'Stay there,' he said, when she started to get up. 'I'll get them.'

'They should be on the top shelf.'

'Are you okay, Nanna?' asked Nicky, as Matt released the childproof lock on the cupboard.

'Yes, darling. Just a little pain.'

Matt reached for the packets he needed, glancing over to see the strained smile his mother tried to give Nicky for reassurance. 'Any other symptoms, Mum? Dizziness? Nausea?'

His fingers fumbled briefly with the sealed end of the aspirin box. Another deep breath to steady himself.

'A—a bit of nausea. And I've got such a headache.'

'That'll probably be the angina meds you took earlier.' A car hooted as he crushed one of the tablets into water. 'Nicky, Davey's mum is here. Can you ask her to come in for a minute, please? Don't forget to take your sports bag.'

'Sure, Dad.' After another quick worried look at Doreen, Nicky set off at a run.

'Drink this.' Matt handed the glass to his mother who swallowed the contents with a small grimace. 'Okay. Now these, one to start with.' He handed her the nitroglycerin tablets.

Once a tablet was tucked under her tongue, he put his arm around her waist. He wanted to stop and hug her and tell her how much he loved her. But she needed him to be a doctor now, not her son. 'Let's get you over to the sofa. You'll be more comfortable.'

'Oh, dear.' Doreen got to her feet and shuffled the few steps. 'I'm sure it'll go away in a minute.'

'Sure to.' He settled her in a semi-reclining position.

Davey's mother appeared a moment later with the boys hovering anxiously behind her. Matt outlined the situation and arranged for Nicky to stay with them after the game. To Nicky, he said, 'I'm not going to be able to come to the game today, okay?'

'Oh, but…I think it's easing already,' said Doreen faintly.

'Of course, Dad.' Nicky gave him a man-to-man look. 'You need to look after Nanna. I understand.'

'Good boy.' He ruffled his son's hair.

After they'd gone, he took Doreen's blood pressure and pulse, recording the readings. 'How are you feeling?'

'A bit better. I'm sure it'll go completely in a few more minutes.' She smiled, obviously relieved. 'I'm sorry to cause such a fuss.'

'Hey, it's not a problem. I need something from the car so you rest here. I'll only be a moment.'

'Okay.'

Matt returned to the kitchen and unpacked the portable ECG unit, getting out a set of disposable electrodes and unravelling the leads. 'I'm going to hook you up for a few minutes.'

'This isn't really necessary, is it?' said Doreen.

'Humour me. I need the practice.' He peeled the backing off one of the electrodes as he explained where he needed to place them. Doreen obligingly pulled the top of her knitted shirt across so he could stick one high on each side of her chest.

With the third electrode stuck low on the ribs beneath her left arm, Matt attached the leads and switched on the unit. Narrow graph paper began smoothly feeding out, lines wriggling across the tiny squares.

'Well?' She craned her neck to look. 'What's the verdict? Will I live?'

'Highly likely. But we'll take a run into Hamilton to get this checked anyway.' The trace wasn't overtly that of a myocardial infarct but it was abnormal enough that he wanted a more experienced eye to look it over. And he'd be happier with a three-plane picture from the hospital's twelve-lead ECG.

'Oh, no. Matt! What about your plans for the day? Darling,

you have so little time for yourself. And aren't you taking Caitlin to watch the boys today?'

'She'll understand.'

'But I've got things to do for my birthday next weekend.' A distinctly mutinous gleam lit her eyes.

He allowed himself a small smile. If she was arguing with him, she must be feeling better. 'Hospital first. Everything else can wait.'

'Will you at least ring Caitlin?'

'When we've got you tucked up in hospital. Do you want your purse?'

'But—'

'Caitlin will understand,' he repeated. 'You know she will. She'd be the first person to tell me to look after you.'

He knew it was true. The more he knew of Caitlin the more sure he was they had something special. He was going to push their relationship harder once Doreen was back on her feet. Life was too short. Whatever was holding Caitlin back needed to be out in the open. Once he knew what it was he would deal with it.

'The hospital is far too busy for us to worry them with a little bit of indigestion.'

'That's what the hospital is there for and they'll be delighted if you turn out to be a false alarm. They've got more sensitive ECG equipment and they'll be able to take blood tests.' He dropped her bag on her lap and scooped her up, ignoring her indignant gasp. 'And that's where I want you to be.'

'Matthew Gardiner. Put me down this instant.'

'You've had a few angina attacks lately and I'd like them investigated.' He ignored her protests, elbowing his way through the screen door. 'This is only going to short-circuit your specialist appointment by a few weeks.'

'What about my things?' she demanded, as he crossed the verandah and negotiated the steps. 'You know I hate wearing hospital gowns.'

'You can make a list of what you want on the way there. For now, your medication's all you need and we have that here,' said Matt, recognising her complaints for the distractions that they were. He set her on her feet and opened the passenger door. 'In you get.'

'You're a bit of a bully, pushing your poor mother around like this.'

'Yeah, I know.' He helped her into the seat. 'I love you, too.'

Once he was on the road, Matt radioed ahead to the emergency department.

'Dr Matt Gardiner here. Could I speak to the cardiac registrar, please? I have a patient with chest pain. Over.'

A few minutes later a different voice sounded in his ear. 'Matt, Sarah Stewart here. How can I help?'

'Sarah, I'm on the road to Hamilton with my mother. She's having chest pains that have been going on for twenty minutes now. Some relief with nitroglycerin. I ran an ECG and there's some arrhythmia but no clear pattern. I'd feel a lot happier to have you look at her. Her angina's been less stable for the last few weeks.'

'What's your ETA?'

'Twenty minutes.'

'Copy that. We'll be expecting you.'

They had a smooth run through to the hospital. A nurse with a wheelchair took Doreen straight through to a cubicle. Matt followed and helped settle his mother on the gurney in one of the despised gowns. Sarah Stewart arrived moments later with a nurse pushing an ECG unit on a trolley.

He stood back, making a few pertinent comments while Sarah took a comprehensive history and explained to Doreen how they were going to treat her case. An ECG, blood tests for cardiac enzymes, an overnight stay at least.

'Matt, please go and ring Caitlin,' said Doreen as Sarah tightened the tourniquet around her arm. 'I feel awful about ruining your date for today.'

'Don't. Your health is much more important.'

'We'll look after Doreen, Matt.' Sarah grinned up at him then exchanged a conspiratorial look with his mother. 'You go and make your phone call so I can pump your mum for the juicy details.'

'Okay, okay.' He raised his hands in mock surrender. 'I won't be long.'

'Take your time, dear. Sarah and I will manage very well,' said Doreen, a cheeky grin creasing her pale face.

Matt walked slowly outside, feeling battered now that the emergency was safely in the hands of the cardiac team. His mother was such a precious part of his tiny family. He didn't want to lose her.

He took out his mobile phone and dialled Caitlin's number.

'Garrangay Veterinary Clinic.'

'Caitlin.' He took a deep breath and closed his eyes, realising for the first time how much he needed to talk to her.

'Matt? What's wrong? You sound awful.'

'We're going to have to cancel today. I'm at the hospital with Mum.'

'Doreen's in hospital? Oh, no.' Her concern was like instant balm. 'What's happened? Is it her heart?'

'Yes.'

'I'm coming in.'

'There's nothing you can do.' Even as he said the words he wondered at his perversity. He wanted her here. Fiercely. Yet he was trying to put her off. 'She won't be allowed visitors for a while.'

'I just want to be there, Matt. I'm leaving now.'

'Okay.' He swallowed around the hot lump in his throat.

'You're in the emergency department?'

'Yes.'

'See you soon.'

After she'd hung up he leaned back against the wall. Caitlin was on her way. The thought bolstered him. His heart swelled with emotion. She cared about his family. She cared about him. Enough to stay in Garrangay? He was beginning to hope so.

Thirty minutes later a nurse came through to Doreen's cubicle to let him know Caitlin had arrived. When he went out to the waiting room, she was sitting on the edge of a chair, her hands clenched on top of her handbag. As soon as she saw him she was on her feet, her arms opening to envelop him.

'Thank you for coming in.'

Holding her as tightly as she clutched him, Matt felt like he'd come home. He leaned into the embrace. This was the place he wanted to be. With his face buried in the crook of her neck, he breathed deeply, filling himself with her. With Caitlin beside him he could face the future. Whatever happened, he would be able to go on if she was there. Her hands began a soothing caress over the tense muscles of his back.

He lifted his head and saw the tears on her cheeks.

'She's going to be fine.' He cupped her face, wiping away the moisture with his thumbs. 'The cardiologist said it was a minor infarct. They're running some tests now to see if she needs a stent. We got treatment started quickly so there's every chance she'll make a full recovery.'

'Thank goodness.' She burrowed back into his shoulder.

Words of commitment trembled on his tongue, but he held them back. His emotions were so raw and needy. He wanted to pin Caitlin down, make her say she wanted to be with him, to be with them. But it wouldn't be fair to take advantage of her in a situation like this. She was too kind. He knew his desperation would make it hard for her to say no. They had things to talk about first and this wasn't the time.

Instead, he absorbed the comfort of holding her close, feeling the way she fitted into his arms, near his heart.

He'd wait a little longer.

But not too long.

CHAPTER SEVENTEEN

'You're not to treat me like an invalid,' said Doreen, sitting at the outdoor table a few evenings later. 'My cardiologist said it was important for me to keep active. I'll be sensible and rest when I need to.'

'Yes, but it won't do you any harm to be on light duties and we don't want to put your new stent under any more pressure than necessary.' Matt flipped the marinated chicken kebabs and rissoles that were sizzling on the hot plate. 'Besides, I'm enjoying teaching Caitlin the finer points of the great Australian barbecue.'

'Really. I would never have noticed.' The wealth of good-natured irony in his mother's voice was hard to miss. But, thankfully, whatever doubts she'd had about him and Caitlin seemed to have gone now.

He'd just finished arranging the cooked kebabs on a platter when the back door swung open. Salad bowl in hand, Caitlin held the screen for Nicky, who was carrying bread and serviettes.

'Good timing.' He arrived at the table at the same time, catching her eye as they arranged the food. The faint rosy glow that tinted her cheeks delighted him.

He could get used to having her around permanently. Who was he kidding? He was *desperate* to have her around permanently. All he had to do was get to the bottom of the resistance he felt from her and convince her to stay. He was sure they had something special, something that was worth taking a risk on.

He trusted her and that was a huge step forward to him. It proved he'd got past Sophie's infidelity.

He was ready to move on. Oh, how he was ready to move on. The dinner-table conversation flowed around him as he thought about when he'd kissed her. Blisteringly hot, intense kisses.

She'd been marvellous over the past few days, stepping in to help whenever she could. Today he'd been free to drive into Hamilton to collect Doreen because Caitlin had picked Nicky up from school.

'I saw Spotty at the clinic today.' Nicky's words interrupted Matt's thoughts. 'He's better, isn't he, Caitlin?'

'He is, yes.'

'Oh, wonderful news,' said Doreen. 'When do you think he can come home?'

'Whenever you're ready. But I can keep him at the clinic longer if you need me to.'

'Keep him at the clinic.'

Matt spoke at the same time as Doreen said, 'Bring him home.'

'It's grand to see you're in agreement, then.' Caitlin looked from one to the other with a grin.

'Bring him home,' Doreen said, her eyes turned to Matt in appeal.

'Yes!' Nicky grinned triumphantly.

Matt's smile was resigned. 'Are you sure he won't be too much for you, Mum?'

'No, he'll be fine. Besides, Nicky will look after him, won't you, dear?' Doreen switched her gaze to Caitlin and said casually, 'Does that mean you'll be able to move back, too, Caitlin?'

'Oh, um, no. It…it's easier for me to stay at the clinic. In case of an emergency. Or something.' She couldn't come back to living under the same roof as Matt now that things had changed between them. It'd be sheer torture to know that he was sleeping in the room above hers. So close, so tempting. Utterly impossible.

But the question made her wonder what she would do when Bob was ready to take over the practice. She'd be effectively homeless unless she came back to the bed and breakfast. She risked a glance at Matt and intercepted a lazy, knowing smile.

'Dad? Phone.' Nicky clattered his knife and fork onto his plate.

'I'd better get that.' Matt stood. 'Excuse me.'

Caitlin watched him walk into the house. Once Bob came back there was really no reason why she couldn't plan on going back to Melbourne. Once she'd told Doreen…. But how could she tell her aunt now while she was convalescing? With the stent in she should be strong enough…

'Can I be excused too, please?' said Nicky. 'I've finished all my salad.'

'Of course, dear,' said Doreen. There was a short companionable silence. 'It's nice to be back home. I haven't told Matt this but…when we first went to hospital I did wonder if I would be coming home.'

Caitlin's hands tightened on her arms. 'It must have been frightening for you.' *For all of us.*

'Yes. There are so many things I still want to do. One of them is my seventieth birthday on Saturday. You are coming, aren't you?'

'Of course. I wouldn't miss it for the world.'

Doreen nodded as though satisfied. 'Gary's come through the bone-marrow transplant with flying colours. Sally told me Bob's thinking of coming home on Monday.'

'Monday?' So soon. Bob had rung her a few times but hadn't put any time frame on his return. An odd panic gripped her. She hadn't even come close to achieving what she needed to do in Garrangay. And now time was running out.

'Will you stay on, do you think?'

Will you want me to once I've told you about your brother?

'I—I'm not sure what I'll do, Doreen.'

'What about you and Matt?'

Caitlin's heart skipped a beat, her mouth dry. For the life of her, she didn't know what to say.

'I'm sorry, dear. I shouldn't interfere…but with this latest episode I'd love to see Matt settled with someone who'll put him and Nicky first in the ways that count.'

Did her aunt see her as that person? It was such an honour and such a weight of responsibility. A huge ball of tearful guilt and longing and love clogged her throat, making it impossible to speak.

'Family's important to Matt, even more so because of where he's come from,' said Doreen, looking at her anxiously. 'I see the way you look at him. You love him, don't you?'

'I do…have feelings for him, yes.' Her voice was hoarse and tight on the wishy-washy words. But her heart was too vulnerable to let her answer more honestly.

Doreen reached out to grasp Caitlin's hand. The older woman's blue-grey eyes were dark. 'Don't leave things unsaid until it's too late, Caitlin.'

Caitlin hesitated. This seemed like such a good lead in to talking about her father, his apology. Almost as though Doreen knew, was giving her permission to break the sad news. But with her aunt still recovering from her heart attack…. Uncertainty held back the half-formed words still on her tongue.

'There are too many things I wish I'd said. We should tell the people we love how precious they are.' Sadness passed over Doreen's face like a bleak shadow. 'We don't always get a second chance.'

'Doreen, I—'

The screen door squeaked open and she swallowed the rest of her sentence.

'Another RSVP for Saturday night, Mum,' said Matt as he came back to the table. 'Remind me again just how many people you invited to this shindig.'

The moment for confiding was gone. A sharp stab of disappointment sliced at her. Would she regret missing this opportunity? Or find another time as good? Somehow she'd have to make one—and soon. Bob was coming back next week. Time was running out.

A job with a view to a partnership in the veterinary practice.... *A chance to stay in Garrangay.* Caitlin's mind whirled with possibilities after Bob's phone call. He'd rung again just after she'd finished the Saturday morning clinic.

Everything she wanted was within her reach. Security. Family. Maybe even the man she loved.

The people, the place, the way of life here in Garrangay had seeped into her, bringing an unfamiliar sense of belonging. *Needs that she'd never acknowledged had been soothed. Empty spaces in her heart and soul had been filled.*

Paradise...except for her secret. Now, with so much else at stake, her deception seemed huge, unforgivable. She'd lied, by omission, to the people she loved. Her reasons for keeping quiet had made perfect sense earlier. She'd been waiting for the right moment. Excuses to delay had been easy to find—not wanting to hurt her aunt, choking on her own unexpected emotion, seeing how things worked out with Matt, Doreen's heart attack.

Disturbed by her thoughts, Caitlin shoved open the car door and scrambled out to stand in the early afternoon sunshine. In front of her, the elaborate wrought-iron gates of the Garrangay cemetery stood open, rows of graves stretching across the small well-tended yard. She'd stopped to have a look but now she was here she felt oddly reluctant to satisfy her curiosity.

Instead, she looked around at the surrounding paddocks, at the lush green spring growth. The clinic would have its work cut out with overweight, under-exercised ponies in the next few months. She'd already handled several cases of acute laminitis.

To stay or not to stay. Everything depended on how she handled this crisis in her personal life.

Turning slowly to face the cemetery gates, Caitlin sighed. She was here...she had to look.

She found herself wandering the rows, reading the names. Young people and old. Doreen's stories lingered in her mind, fleshing out the names, the connections between families. Her unsuspecting aunt had been more than happy to talk about her research into the family history, to show off the wonderful collection of old, old photographs of her ancestors. Her own ancestors.

She stopped at a polished granite stone and read the words aloud. "'In loving memory of Albert and Frances Brown. Sixth of December. Together always.'"

The anniversary was just under a month away. She realised anew how close to Christmas her grandparents' car accident had been. How much extra grief that must have added to the children they'd left behind. To Doreen, just married and suddenly responsible for her little brother. To Martin, who had been trapped in the vehicle until help had arrived. Too late for his parents. A terrifying experience for a twelve-year-old boy.

She stepped carefully to the head of the grave and crouched to splay her fingers over the smooth surface of the cool stone. There was room for more names. Her father's name belonged here. How would Doreen feel about having her brother added?

'Doreen's parents.'

Caitlin jolted at the sound of Matt's voice, snatching her hand away from the stone. Guilt sent heat surging into her cheeks then, just as fast, it receded, leaving her face cold, almost numb.

'Hey, sorry. You must have been miles away.' He frowned when she stared up at him mutely. 'Caitlin? Are you all right?'

'Yes.' Had that faint croak really come from her? She rose carefully. Her heart thumped in fast, hard beats making her feel sick and giddy.

'We were on our way home from cricket when Nicky spotted your car.'

'Did he?'

He looked back down at the headstone. 'They died in a car accident.'

'I—I know.'

He was standing at the end of the grave, his lips gently tilted at the corners. She should summon up an answering smile, make a disarming comment, move casually away from the grave. Instead, guilt and fear held her paralysed.

Matt's green eyes drifted back to the names on the stone. She watched him, noticing the way the sun caught the golden highlights in his hair, the way he stood, hands tucked into his pockets, relaxed. A sudden chill of inevitability swept over her, spinning her world out of control.

She didn't want to lose him.

Powerless to deflect the thoughts she could almost see coalescing in his mind, she waited. His lips parted and she watched them form the words she was dreading.

'Caitlin Butler-Brown,' he said slowly. 'I've just realised your father would have been a Brown.'

'Yes.'

'Wouldn't it be funny if you were related?'

The words hung between them for long silent moments. A shadow passed over the sun, robbing Caitlin of its precious radiant warmth, leaving her frozen.

'Would it?' She forced the question past the tight, gravelly lump in her throat.

He stared at her, his green eyes narrowing as he began to absorb the possibility.

'It's not a coincidence that you were travelling this way.' It was half statement, half question.

'No.'

He tilted his chin slightly towards the headstone, his eyes still fixed to hers. 'You're...related?'

'Yes.'

'How?'

She clasped her hands tightly. 'These are my grandparents.'

'Then you must be…Martin's daughter?'

She took a deep breath, hoping it would steady her for the developing crisis. 'I am, yes.'

The silence was terrible, a growing impenetrable wall, severing the weeks of happiness and connection between them. Sorrow congealed as a pain in her chest. Her heart a leaden thing beating from habit when she knew it should have been shrivelling and dying.

The sun popped back out, suddenly brightening colours, incongruously cheery. Its warmth on her skin merely exacerbated the bone-deep chill of her body.

'Why are you here? What do you want?' His face was hard, his eyes as flat and cold as his voice.

'I came because I want to know about my father's family.' She tilted her chin defiantly.

'You want to know—' He bit off the rest of the sentence and spun away from her as he thrust his fingers through his hair.

Caitlin looked at his rigid back, waited numbly for him to speak again. When he turned back, his face was drawn, his lips set in a straight uncompromising line. 'Why don't you ask him?'

'I-I can't. He passed away. He never talked about his family,' she said, struggling with a sudden need to cry. 'Until he was dying.'

A spasm of despair twisted his features. She was fiercely glad he uttered no words of condolence. Any indication of softness from him would have broken her fragile poise. But she couldn't help longing for a tiny sign that he would be able to forgive her. There was nothing except the coldness and anger that she deserved.

After a long moment he said, 'Doreen is going to be devastated by this. Martin chose not to let his sister be a part of his life. But now you're here to make her a part of his death.'

'I thought she should know, that she'd want to know.' Her mouth felt stiff and uncooperative.

'Why?'

'Da wanted to apologise to her. I promised him I'd come and see her, speak to her.'

'Did you?' His lip curled in disdain. 'And you're here to salve his conscience? Or your own?'

Caitlin was stricken by his unrelenting harshness. Nausea threatened with spasms that cramped her stomach. She swallowed the bile that rose in her throat and stared at him in silence. His reaction was even worse than she'd anticipated.

'Why haven't you said anything before now?'

'I haven't known how to. I thought, by getting to know Doreen, I'd find the right way to tell her.' She made a small gesture of defeat with her hands. 'I...I haven't.'

His eyes closed, Matt massaged his forehead with the fingers of one hand as though trying to rub away an overwhelming pain.

'Hi, Caitlin. Look what I found.'

She dragged her gaze down to Nicky's outstretched hand. A long green praying mantis sat motionless in his palm.

'He's beautiful.' She managed a small smile.

'Dad, can I take him home for show and tell on Monday?'

'Sure. Why don't you wait in the car, Nicky? I'll be right there.' When his son had gone, Matt turned back to her. 'We need to talk about this. *Before* you say anything to Mum. Do you understand me?'

She felt beaten, broken. 'Yes,' she managed.

He nodded once before spinning on his heel and striding down the grassy path.

She waited until he was gone, his car out of sight, before lowering herself slowly to sit on the edge of the concrete. It was a long time before she could find the strength to totter back to her car. Going through the motions of finding the keys, starting the vehicle, took every ounce of her energy.

Numb with a grief too deep for simple tears, she drove back to the clinic. Doreen had said to come early for the birthday party but Caitlin couldn't go to Mill House yet. How was she going to face Matt after what had been said? She'd thought she was so clever, coming to meet her aunt, to learn about her roots. Instead, she'd ended up falling for a man who now wanted nothing to do with her. She had an aunt whom she adored but would hurt dreadfully by revealing their connection. In short, she'd made a bloody mess of things.

Matt drove the car automatically, steering, changing gear, braking. Nicky's chatter filled the empty spaces. All he needed to do was murmur appropriate responses. His mind went over and over what had just taken place.

If only Nicky hadn't spotted Caitlin's car…

If only they hadn't stopped…

If only he hadn't had to learn his perfect woman was hiding a secret that could rip his mother's heart to shreds.

But Nicky *had* seen the car, they *had* stopped. And he'd learned his perfect woman, the woman he trusted, had feet of clay. All that time he'd thought they were building something worthwhile together and she'd been working her own agenda with his family. She'd betrayed him. Possibly even *used* him to gain more access to his foster-mother, her aunt.

She was like Sophie after all. Only this time he felt the perfidy even more sharply.

He loved her. He *loved* her. He'd wanted to make her a part of his family.

She hadn't just betrayed him as a man, she threatened all that was precious to him.

The best he could do was protect and defend what was left. And if that meant shutting Caitlin out, he'd do it. Regardless of how his heart bled at the thought.

CHAPTER EIGHTEEN

CAITLIN let her gaze drift to Matt for the hundredth time. The party had been well under way by the time she'd arrived and he stood behind the barbecue wielding a pair of tongs and laughing at something the woman beside him had said. He looked relaxed and comfortable. Not at all heartbroken.

But, then, she probably didn't either. Even though her spirit was shrivelling, her self-respect had demanded that she cobble the pieces of herself together. Present a reasonable façade. Strange how a person could be in so much pain and yet look perfectly normal.

Even with happy, chattering people surrounding her, she felt desperately isolated. As though she watched a puppet of herself perform socially. Her responses must have been appropriate because people kept smiling at her and she smiled back.

She filed across to the food with everyone else, picking up a plate and helping herself to salads. Everything looked delicious and she wondered how she was going to force any of it into her knotted stomach. A surreptitious glance at her watch confirmed it was still too early to make excuses to leave. The pager at her belt stayed wretchedly silent.

Plate in hand, she wandered through the crowd, exchanging a word here and there. Finally finding a secluded spot in the rustic pergola at the bottom of the garden, she sat her plate on a post and leaned on the rail. The evening sky was a spec-

tacular wash of apricot and gold-etched clouds above the sil-
houette of the Grampians. When she left tomorrow she was
going to miss this view.

Though not half as much as she'd miss the small family
she'd come to love—Doreen, Nicky…Matt. Her heart twisted
painfully as his name reverberated in her mind.

'Caitlin.'

She jolted at the sound of her name, her fingers digging into
the wood reflexively. Taking a deep breath, she turned her
head slightly. 'Matt.'

'I saw you walk down here.' He came to stand beside her.
'We need to talk.'

How could she bear it? She felt her chin quiver and hoped
it was too dark for him to see her weakness. 'Do we?'

'I—' He turned away abruptly, spearing his fingers into his
hair. 'Don't tell Mum why you're here.' The plea came out in a
rush.

'Don't you think she has a right to know?' How composed
she sounded. Unbelievable when she felt so close to shattering.

'Yes, she does.' He spun to face her. 'But I can't bear to have
her hurt by this.'

The anguish in his voice pierced straight to her soul. She
looked down at her hands clutching the rail. 'I wouldn't do
anything to harm Doreen, you know that.'

'Then you won't tell her?'

Each word hammered his distrust home in a painful tattoo
in Caitlin's vulnerable heart. Only the wood she held so tightly
held her trembling frame upright.

She looked at him. The man she loved, the man she had to
leave. Her hope for the future died. 'I won't, no.'

He shut his eyes, relief plain on his face. He hadn't been
sure of her response—somehow knowing that made her feel
even worse.

'Thank you, Caitlin. I understand how difficult this must
be for you.'

'Do you, now?' she said, unable to keep the edge out of her voice. She felt an inappropriate urge to laugh but didn't dare. Tears were too close. He understood nothing. How could he when she struggled to understand it herself? 'How perceptive of you.'

'Doreen told me Bob's offered you a job, maybe even—'

'Don't worry,' she interrupted. He had what he wanted. Why couldn't he just leave her alone? 'I've turned it down.'

'Caitlin—'

'I think we've said all that needs saying, Matt.' Desperately scanning the gaily lit garden party beyond the perimeter of the pergola, she latched onto a familiar figure. 'If you'll excuse me, I can see that Joy Warren's arrived. I need to speak with her.'

Restless, Matt strode down the now deserted garden. Sweet perfume from the flowering pittosporum mingled with the scent of freshly mown grass in the still night air.

The evening had gone well. No surprise. Doreen had been in her element. His concerns about her overdoing things had been unfounded, though he'd packed her off to bed as soon as the last guest left. An army of willing helpers had already tidied up and the dishwasher was gurgling through the last of the crockery.

Caitlin had left early. She'd managed to slip away while he wasn't watching—an impressive feat since he'd hardly taken his eyes off her.

As he neared the pergola, moonlight glinted on a plate that had been left on the post. He looked at the untouched food, re-membering how Caitlin had fled after their brief discussion.

Had he made a colossal mistake? He'd begun to think so almost as soon as he'd spoken to her. Doreen *did* have a right to know about her estranged brother. His motives for keeping it from her didn't seem to stand up to scrutiny at this late hour.

He'd been furious when he'd found out Caitlin's purpose for being in Garrangay. He hated the thought of Doreen being hurt. Fear and anger had pushed him to demand Caitlin's silence and her defiance had folded. She cared about Doreen. About him. She was prepared to put her own needs aside rather than cause him pain.

He hadn't given her the same consideration.

After a lifetime of nomadic existence, she wanted stability. She'd found it in her work in Melbourne. But when she wanted to reach out, find her roots, find family, he'd stopped her.

He'd perceived her need as a threat to his security, his family's security, and he'd reacted to contain it. And he'd hurt her dreadfully in the process. Her pain had been clear in her eyes, her face, her demeanour.

He'd been angry with her. Seen her secret identity as a betrayal after making him love her.

But now he'd had a chance to calm down he realised he had to make it right, help her find a way to tell Doreen the truth. Even if he'd wrecked his chances of a future with Caitlin, he had to make sure she connected with her family.

Too late tonight, much as he was tempted to go right this minute. First thing in the morning, before he took Nicky to pony club.

'Haley? Is Caitlin there, please?'

Matt's voice on speakerphone sliced through Caitlin's concentration. She took a sharp breath in and then forced all of her attention back to the dog on the operating table. Years of training prevented the quiver in her mind from reaching the fingers performing the femoral-artery repair.

'Yes, she is, Matt,' said Haley. 'But she can't come to the phone right now. We're in theatre with an emergency case.'

There was a silence.

'Can you ask her to ring me when she's finished? It's important, Haley. I need to speak her as soon as possible. I'm not at home so she'll have to ring me on my mobile.'

'No worries, Matt.'

'Thanks. I'll let you get back to it.'

A moment later the veterinary nurse returned to the other side of the table.

'Could you retract that muscle, please, Haley?'

A gleaming tool moved into position, improving her view of the damage. The dog was lucky to be alive. If the owner hadn't been there when the bull had gored her pet, the animal wouldn't have survived. She tidied up the torn tissue.

'He's gorgeous, isn't he?'

'Who? Suction, please, Haley.' The nozzle moved into position, noisily removing the fluid pooled at the bottom of the wound.

'Matt, of course. It's so cool that you guys are going out together. He deserves to be happy.'

'Mmm. Let's unclamp.' She watched the clip being released, her hands poised to intervene if there was a problem. The artery swelled, turning dark red as the blood flowed back into the lumen. The suture line held, no sign of leakage.

'Good work, Dr Butler-Brown.'

Caitlin grinned. 'Thank you, Nurse Simpson. Let's check the intestines.'

It was another hour before they could close up. In the kidney dish beside the table lay a length of resected bowel that had been too damaged to repair.

She stripped off her bloodied gloves before gathering the groggy boxer in her arms. Haley collected the drip and opened the door into the cage area.

'Bless you for coming in to help with this, Haley,' she said as she settled the heavily bandaged animal on the bedding. 'I couldn't have operated without you.'

'I was glad to have an excuse to leave the house. Cam's repainting the lounge. That man adores renovating as much as I hate it.' Haley chuckled.

'Oh, dear. I *was* going to suggest I'd finish up if you wanted to go home.' Caitlin stood to adjust the drip and slanted a smile at her assistant.

'I've got a better idea,' said Haley. 'Why don't I finish up while you go and ring Matt?'

'Mmm. I'd appreciate it if you would.' Guilt pinched at Caitlin. She hadn't told Haley she was leaving today. The words wouldn't come. She promised herself she'd ring to apologise when she was safely back in Melbourne.

'You've got his number?'

'Oh, yes. I have his number.' But she wouldn't be using it. What could he want to speak to her about? Whatever it was, she didn't want to hear it. If that smacked of cowardice, it was too bad. The previous two encounters with him had left her wounded and fragile. She'd taken as much as she could.

Bob was back. Haley had gone home.

And Caitlin was on her way. Just a quick stop at Mill House. She had to say goodbye to Doreen.

Please, let Matt still be at pony club.

Her aunt was in the kitchen, setting scones out on a floured oven tray with quick, efficient movements.

'Doreen? I…I'm heading off today.'

'Where to, dear? Have you been over to see that new gallery yet?'

'No. Doreen…I'm leaving, going back to Melbourne.'

'You're leaving? But…' The sentence trailed off and Doreen's blue-grey eyes went wide with shock as she stood, a lump of scone dough suspended from floury fingers. 'But I thought… Sally told me Bob was going to offer you a position in the practice.'

'He did. But I'm a city girl.' Caitlin forced her wooden face into what she hoped would be a reassuring smile. 'Being here, working in a country practice, has been grand. But I need to get serious and find a job.'

'What about you and Matt?'

'We've spoken, said what needs to be said.' She fluttered her hands, seeking to distract Doreen from the quaver in her voice.

'But…Caitlin…there are some things that I…that I have to ask you.' She looked at the dough still hanging from her hand and slowly lowered it to the baking tray as she spoke. 'I've put it off because I thought there was plenty of time, but now… Let me make coffee.'

Caitlin glanced at her watch surreptitiously. She wanted, *needed*, to be gone before Matt came back to the house. 'I should really—'

'The jug's just boiled.' Doreen quickly rinsed her fingers and dried them on her apron before collecting a couple of mugs.

'There you are,' she said a few moments later as she placed two steaming mugs of coffee on the table.

'Thanks.' Caitlin sank onto a chair, frowning as she watched her aunt add spoonful after spoonful of sugar to her mug. The agitated clink of metal on pottery filled the silence.

'Doreen?'

'There's no easy way for me to say this so I might as well just come out and say it.' Her aunt fixed her with an intense scrutiny. 'There are times when I think I must be mad for thinking…. But then something…'

Caitlin interlaced her fingers and held them tightly in her lap. As fragile as she was feeling right now, she didn't think she could bear a well-meant heart-to-heart about Matt and their disastrous relationship.

'You're my brother's daughter, aren't you?'

Caitlin's mouth opened then closed. Finally she managed, 'I—I…. What makes you…?' She swallowed. What could she say? She'd made a promise. But she couldn't lie to her aunt. 'Oh, God. Doreen.'

'I've been waiting for you to say something.'

Hope vied with guilt in Caitlin's reeling mind. 'Have you? H-how did you…?'

'How did I work it out? I think I knew the first moment I saw you. You have his eyes and every now and then…your expression is pure Marty.' She shook her head slightly, a reminiscent smile playing around her mouth. After a long moment, she asked, 'How is my brother?'

'I'm so sorry, Doreen.' Quick, hot tears welled in Caitlin's eyes. She pressed her fingers briefly to her lips and took a deep breath. 'He—he…'

'He's gone, isn't he?'

'Y-yes. He passed away a year ago.' Her voice felt rusty and harsh in her throat. 'He had cancer.'

'Oh, Caitlin.'

She found herself enfolded in a warm embrace and Doreen's sobs joined her own. After a few minutes she pulled back, digging in a pocket for a handkerchief to blow her nose. Her aunt did the same.

'My baby brother was a father.' Wonder filled Doreen's voice. 'And look at you. You're gorgeous and clever. He must have been so proud of you.'

Fresh tears flooded her eyes. 'I think so. I hope so.'

'There's so much I want to know about you and Marty. So many questions I want to ask.'

'Da wanted to apologize to you for everything and especially for staying away.' She made a small mental apology to Matt. But it felt so good, so right, to finally be saying these things. 'I think if he'd been well enough, he'd have come to see you.'

'Poor Marty. Did he tell you why he ran away?'

Caitlin shook her head.

'We had terrible fights over his schooling after our parents were killed. I was so set on him completing his education.'

'He said he knew you'd only wanted the best for him but he was too bloody-minded.' Caitlin took her aunt's hand, wanting to soothe away the pain. 'He told me he'd done you terrible harm and he didn't know how to make amends.'

Doreen squeezed Caitlin's fingers. 'After he left, I lost my baby. It was late in the pregnancy and I started haemorrhaging. They had to operate to save me. Marty rang while I was in hospital and Pete told him what had happened.' She seemed to be gathering herself to finish. 'Marty never came home again. Never got in touch.'

Her smile was tremulous. 'Pete and I started fostering soon afterwards. I think I hoped that someone would take Marty under their wing.'

'Like you were doing for others with your fostering.'

'Yes, exactly. We had so many wonderful young lives in our home.'

Caitlin remembered the haunting picture of an intense, green-eyed youth that Doreen had showed her. 'And Matt was one of them?'

'Yes, he was a darling boy. We would have adopted him if his mother had let us. She was a drug addict, you know?'

'He told me.'

'Matt told you that?' Doreen sounded surprised. 'Drug addiction is a terrible thing, and not just for the addict. That poor little boy. All we could do was make sure he had somewhere to come when she went off the rails. She loved him enough not to take him away from Garrangay but not enough to stay away from drugs.'

'You gave him an anchor when he needed it. He loves you very much.'

'He's a man with a lot of love to give, my dear.'

Perhaps he was. But none of it would ever be for her, not now. Grief for what might have been crushed her heart all over again.

'I'm so glad you came, Caitlin. Oh, there are so many things I want to ask you and here you are going back to Melbourne. Are you sure you can't stay longer?'

Caitlin hesitated briefly. 'Not this time, Doreen. I'm so sorry. But we'll stay in touch and I promise I'll be back as soon as…as soon as I can.'

As soon as she knew she could face Matt without breaking down. As soon as her battered heart could cope. Too much to hope that it would mend, but a little time away from him might start the healing process. She wasn't going to let the thought of seeing him stop her from spending time with her aunt, not now that everything was out in the open.

'There's something I'd like you to have. It belonged to my mother, your grandmother.'

Caitlin watched Doreen hurry out of the room. She really needed to start her journey but it was beyond her to cut short these precious moments with her aunt.

Caitlin wasn't going to ring him, Matt was sure of it. He strode across the veterinary clinic car park and thumped on the back door.

'Bob!' The shock of seeing the vet took Matt a long second to assimilate. 'You're back?'

'Hello, Matt. Come in.'

'No, I…. Caitlin?' His mind felt sluggish and his feet stayed rooted to the steps. 'Where is she?'

'Gone.'

Panic punched him in the gut. 'Gone? Where?'

'Back to Melbourne. It was the strangest thing. She—'

'When?' Matt forced the question past numb lips.

'About half an hour ago. Didn't she—?'

'Thanks. Sorry, Bob. I have to go. We'll catch up later.' Matt ran to the car. She was going to leave without saying goodbye to him…without saying goodbye to Doreen and Nicky. Because of him. He'd run her off. He'd been such an idiot.

An *eejit*.

Just thinking of the way she pronounced the insult made him want to groan. God, he had to find her. She could call him all the names under the sun as long as she stayed.

He yanked open the car door. How was he going to find her? Would she take the direct route back to Melbourne?

'She said something about calling at Mill House to see Doreen,' yelled Bob, from the back doorstep.

'Thanks.' Matt stabbed the key into the ignition.

As he drove home, he rehearsed the words he wanted to say to Caitlin. Tried to imagine her response.

The more he'd thought about it, the worse his interference seemed. Was she going to be able to forgive him for the things he'd said?

Caitlin had a right to share her grief about her father with someone who'd care. He'd denied two of the most important people in his life the opportunity to comfort each other.

Matt had suffered loss in his life but Doreen and Pete had always been there. A solid foundation, a place to lay his sorrows, to seek consolation. People, family, who accepted him no matter what.

Caitlin had no one. Her mother sounded distant in more ways than one. And now, in his selfishness, in his concern that his life didn't change, he'd denied her access to her aunt.

Matt smiled grimly. Once Doreen heard about the way he'd treated her niece, he was going to get a thorough ticking off.

Doreen was getting older. He had to acknowledge that he was going to lose her one day. Perhaps that was another reason why he wanted to hold onto things as they were for as long as possible. But change was inevitable.

Relief shuddered through him when he saw Caitlin's little MG parked at the side of Mill House. He wasn't too late to speak to her. Would he be too late to salvage their relationship? He didn't know but he was going to give it a damned good try.

His mother and Caitlin were hugging each other in the hallway as he came through the front door. He knew the moment she realised he was there. A shudder of shock ran through her body and the colour drained from her face.

'Oh, Matt. You're home. Thank heavens,' said Doreen, relief plain on her face. 'I didn't want Caitlin to leave without seeing you.'

'No. I don't want that either,' he said softly, placing his keys on the stand as he walked towards them. 'We have things to discuss. Caitlin has some things to tell you.'

'I know. She's my niece, Matt.'

His footsteps faltered for a moment as the words sank in.

'She told you.' A tiny dart of disappointment needled him. Caitlin had broken her promise after all. But what did it matter? He wanted the truth to come out.

Out of the corner of his eye he saw Caitlin stiffen.

'She didn't have to.' His mother was radiant with happiness. 'I've suspected from the very first day.'

'You knew? All this time?' He stared at Doreen. 'Why didn't you say something?'

'I nearly did. It seems stupid now that I didn't.' She turned back to Caitlin. 'But I was afraid in case I scared you away by prying. I thought you'd say something if I gave you enough time.'

Matt cleared his throat. 'She would have, Mum. I told her not to.'

'You told her not to?' Doreen looked up at him in obvious confusion. 'Why would you do that?'

'I was trying to protect you.' He ran a hand around the back of his neck, feeling the tension in the muscles. What an arrogant fool he'd been to think he knew best.

'But, darling, of course I'd want to know about Marty. His leaving has always been like a hole in my heart.' Doreen's face creased in a look of mingled reproach and affection.

'I know.' His gaze moved back to Caitlin. *A hole in the heart.* That was exactly what he was going to have if he couldn't convince the woman he loved to stay.

After a short pause, his mother said, 'Yes. I can see that you do.'

'I need to talk to Caitlin, Mum.'

'Yes, and mind you do a good job of it.' She took Caitlin's hands and held them. 'Let him grovel, Caitlin, dear. Something tells me he's earned it.'

The silence, after Doreen walked away, seemed to take on a life of its own. Caitlin cautiously drew in a deep breath, needing the oxygen in her lungs but loath to disturb their tableau. She'd thought earlier she couldn't feel any worse.

She was wrong.

'Caitlin?' Matt's voice was low and charged with emotion. When his hand reached towards her, she pulled back, wrapping her arms around her waist, holding herself tight. If he touched her now she'd surely shatter. After a moment he lowered his arm to his side. 'Come through to the study.'

She stood her ground. 'I kept my promise to you.'

'I know.'

'I'm not sorry Doreen knows the truth.' She had to hold onto that. She had a family. Falling in love with Matt had been an unfortunate detour.

'Neither am I.'

'I— You're not?' She struggled to grasp the meaning of his words. 'Then what else is there to say? I've got a long drive to make, Matt.' She was proud of the way she sounded. Firm, determined. Not like she was falling apart inside.

He moved closer and she stepped back.

'I'd like to get back to Melbourne before it gets too late.'

'Yes, I understand.' He reached past her shoulder. She retreated another step. Two.

'I'll need to do some shopping since I've been away so long. Milk and...' Now she was babbling. That wasn't so good. 'Milk and stuff. Bread. You know.'

'Yes, I know.' His voice was soothing, as though he was trying to calm a skittish animal.

She turned away, took several paces then stopped short as she realised she was standing in the study. There was a small click as the door shut behind her. The tiny sound sent a tremor through her body.

She was alone with him. It took every ounce of self-discipline to quell the urge to bolt. She tightened her arms across her stomach. Whatever he had to say, she would survive and move on.

She *would*. She was strong.

Tilting her chin, she turned to face him. He was standing so close, his expression too gentle, almost…loving. *No, that couldn't be right.* All she knew was if he didn't stop looking at her that way, her bracing internal lecture would be worthless.

'What's so important, then?' she managed through stiff lips.

'I was wrong to stop you talking to Mum about her brother. About your father.' His voice was rough with emotion.

She'd been ready for a fight. His admission knocked the starch out of her. 'Oh.'

'She had a right to know.'

'Oh. Th-thank you.' Caitlin felt she should say more but her mind refused to function.

'I'm sorry.'

'You—you wanted to protect your mother.'

'You're making excuses for me.' He smiled crookedly and reached out slowly, giving her time to move away if she chose. Her breath froze in her chest as he skimmed her ear, tucking away a strand of hair. Taking his time. The expression on his face was so beautiful it brought a lump to her throat. 'It wasn't Mum I was protecting, my darling. It was me. I was afraid.'

'I was afraid, too,' she murmured. His hand rested on her shoulder, the warmth seeping through her. He'd called her his darling. What did it mean? A wayward spark of hope blossomed in her heart. 'I nearly told you why I was here. I didn't know what to do. I was so afraid of hurting Doreen, of hurting all of you.'

'I know. You humbled me when you said you'd walk away rather than cause her pain.' His hand moved to the nape of her neck, the thumb rubbing sensitive skin at her throat. Could he feel the crazy beating of her pulse? She should move away but her brain refused to send the signals to her feet.

'I love you.' His voice was a soft caress.

She gulped in a breath as the meaning of the miraculous words slowly sank in. 'You—you love me?'

'Yes. And I'll tell you every day for the rest of my life if you'll stay here and let me. You belong with me. I want us to be a family,' he murmured, his hands coming up to cup her face.

She stared into the warm green of his eyes. 'I don't know if I'm any good at family. What if I mess up? What if I—?'

'Shh.' His thumbs came up to press against her lips, stopping her words with soft insistence. 'Caitlin, you're already *great* at family. Trust me, darling.'

He placed his lips on hers, spinning her thoughts wildly out of control. She slid her hands around his waist, needing to anchor herself.

'We belong together.'

'Oh, Matt.' She bit her lip. 'I want that so much.'

'Then that's all that matters.' His mouth slanted across hers. 'Marry me.' But he didn't give her a chance to answer, instead leaving her breathless with another kiss. 'We can live in Garrangay.'

'Yes,' she gasped, as his lips pressed to hers again.

'Or wherever you want to.'

'No, nowhere else. Why would I want to leave Garrangay?' She drew back to meet his eyes. 'Everything I need is right here.'

Hope and happiness flared in the deep green. 'You'll stay? You'll marry me?'

'Yes and yes. I love you, Matt Gardiner.'

His arms wrapped around her, scooping her up on his chest so she looked down on his broad grin. 'You won't regret it. I'll make you happy. We'll make you happy.'

She could hardly breathe but she didn't care. She wanted him to hold her like this. Tight to his body, tight in his life. The way she was going to hold him and never let go.

EPILOGUE

SHE was getting *married*. Today. *Now.*

A shiver of delicious terror shuddered along Caitlin's nerves. Marrying Matt was what she wanted more than anything in the world.

So why was she loitering in her room, putting off the moment of facing everyone?

Putting off the moment of facing Matt?

She loved him. She loved his family…her family.

But just because she wanted family, a place to belong, it didn't mean she'd be good at it, good for them. She'd had no practice, no experience at stability. It wasn't just her life that would be affected if she messed up.

She needed to see Matt, talk to him. Draw strength from him. But Doreen had been adamant. Grooms did not see their brides before the wedding—it was bad luck. So he'd been dispatched to stay at Bob and Sally's last night, to be delivered back here in time for the ceremony.

He would be standing out there right now, waiting, wondering what was keeping her. If she didn't unglue her feet, she was in danger of being an unfashionably late bride.

She jumped at a small tap on the door. Doreen must be back to see what the problem was.

'Yes? Come in.' She pinned a smile on her lips.

Nicky's face popped around the edge of the door. 'Hi, Caitlin.'

'Hi, yourself.'

Spotty's head appeared a second later and the dog bounced into the room.

'Sit, Spotty,' Nicky said sternly. The spotted rump immediately plopped to the floor, the tail still wagging frantically, sending vibrations through the lean frame.

'Wow, you've been working hard on those obedience lessons.'

'Spotty learns quick. He's real smart.' Nicky came to stand beside the excited pup.

'And so are you for teaching him.' She looked at him. He was a miniature version of Matt, dressed in a smart dark grey suit and red tie. 'Don't you look grand in your finery, then?'

'Nanna said that, too.' He smiled. 'Dad sent us. He said you might have cold feet.'

Her lips quivered, just a little. 'Did he, now?'

'That means you're scared, doesn't it?'

'That is what it means, yes.'

'But that's silly, isn't it? Why would you be scared 'cos you're marrying Dad? It means you get to live with us for ever and ever.'

Love for her stepson-to-be overflowed from her heart. 'So it does.'

Nicky's face screwed up with concentration. 'And Dad said to say we'd do it one day at a time.'

'When you put it like that, it's quite simple, then, isn't it?' And it was, she realised. 'Your dad's pretty smart, isn't he?'

'Yep. He said you'd understand. So are you coming now? Dad's waiting.'

'Then let's not keep him waiting any longer.' She held her hand out. Nicky's small fingers closed over hers. Spotty seemed to sense they were ready to go and bounded out ahead of them.

She walked through the garden with her escort, peripherally aware of everyone. Matt stood under the rose arch. Her heart squeezed with love as his mouth curved into a secret smile. How could she not love this wonderful, perceptive man? He'd understood, sent his emissaries to help her.

'We got her, Dad. You can get married now.'

'Thank you, Nicky,' Matt said softly, as he exchanged a man-to-man look with his son.

Caitlin watched Nicky and Spotty go to stand by her aunt. When she raised her eyes to her groom she found him watching her, his green eyes filled with love and concern.

'All right, darling?'

'I am, now, yes.'

Warmth and confidence flooded her. She was going to love and be loved by her new family, each and every day for the rest of her life.

MILLS & BOON®
Pure reading pleasure™

MAY 2009 HARDBACK TITLES

ROMANCE

The Greek Tycoon's Blackmailed Mistress	Lynne Graham
Ruthless Billionaire, Forbidden Baby	Emma Darcy
Constantine's Defiant Mistress	Sharon Kendrick
The Sheikh's Love-Child	Kate Hewitt
The Boss's Inexperienced Secretary	Helen Brooks
Ruthlessly Bedded, Forcibly Wedded	Abby Green
The Desert King's Bejewelled Bride	Sabrina Philips
Bought: For His Convenience or Pleasure?	Maggie Cox
The Playboy of Pengarroth Hall	Susanne James
The Santorini Marriage Bargain	Margaret Mayo
The Brooding Frenchman's Proposal	Rebecca Winters
His L.A. Cinderella	Trish Wylie
Dating the Rebel Tycoon	Ally Blake
Her Baby Wish	Patricia Thayer
The Sicilian's Bride	Carol Grace
Always the Bridesmaid	Nina Harrington
The Valtieri Marriage Deal	Caroline Anderson
Surgeon Boss, Bachelor Dad	Lucy Clark

HISTORICAL

The Notorious Mr Hurst	Louise Allen
Runaway Lady	Claire Thornton
The Wicked Lord Rasenby	Marguerite Kaye

MEDICAL™

The Rebel and the Baby Doctor	Joanna Neil
The Country Doctor's Daughter	Gill Sanderson
The Greek Doctor's Proposal	Molly Evans
Single Father: Wife and Mother Wanted	Sharon Archer

0409 Gen Std LP

ROMANCE

The Billionaire's Bride of Vengeance	Miranda Lee
The Santangeli Marriage	Sara Craven
The Spaniard's Virgin Housekeeper	Diana Hamilton
The Greek Tycoon's Reluctant Bride	Kate Hewitt
Nanny to the Billionaire's Son	Barbara McMahon
Cinderella and the Sheikh	Natasha Oakley
Promoted: Secretary to Bride!	Jennie Adams
The Black Sheep's Proposal	Patricia Thayer

HISTORICAL

The Captain's Forbidden Miss	Margaret McPhee
The Earl and the Hoyden	Mary Nichols
From Governess to Society Bride	Helen Dickson

MEDICAL™

Dr Devereux's Proposal	Margaret McDonagh
Children's Doctor, Meant-to-be Wife	Meredith Webber
Italian Doctor, Sleigh-Bell Bride	Sarah Morgan
Christmas at Willowmere	Abigail Gordon
Dr Romano's Christmas Baby	Amy Andrews
The Desert Surgeon's Secret Son	Olivia Gates

0509 Gen Std HB

MILLS & BOON®
Pure reading pleasure™

JUNE 2009 HARDBACK TITLES

ROMANCE

The Sicilian's Baby Bargain	Penny Jordan
Mistress: Pregnant by the Spanish Billionaire	Kim Lawrence
Bound by the Marcolini Diamonds	Melanie Milburne
Blackmailed into the Greek Tycoon's Bed	Carol Marinelli
The Ruthless Greek's Virgin Princess	Trish Morey
Veretti's Dark Vengeance	Lucy Gordon
Spanish Magnate, Red-Hot Revenge	Lynn Raye Harris
Argentinian Playboy, Unexpected Love-Child	Chantelle Shaw
The Savakis Mistress	Annie West
Captive in the Millionaire's Castle	Lee Wilkinson
Cattle Baron: Nanny Needed	Margaret Way
Greek Boss, Dream Proposal	Barbara McMahon
Boardroom Baby Surprise	Jackie Braun
Bachelor Dad on Her Doorstep	Michelle Douglas
Hired: Cinderella Chef	Myrna Mackenzie
Miss Maple and the Playboy	Cara Colter
A Special Kind of Family	Marion Lennox
Hot Shot Surgeon, Cinderella Bride	Alison Roberts

HISTORICAL

The Rake's Wicked Proposal	Carole Mortimer
The Transformation of Miss Ashworth	Anne Ashley
Mistress Below Deck	Helen Dickson

MEDICAL™

Emergency: Wife Lost and Found	Carol Marinelli
A Summer Wedding at Willowmere	Abigail Gordon
The Playboy Doctor Claims His Bride	Janice Lynn
Miracle: Twin Babies	Fiona Lowe

MILLS & BOON®

Pure reading pleasure™

JUNE 2009 LARGE PRINT TITLES

ROMANCE

The Ruthless Magnate's Virgin Mistress	Lynne Graham
The Greek's Forced Bride	Michelle Reid
The Sheikh's Rebellious Mistress	Sandra Marton
The Prince's Waitress Wife	Sarah Morgan
The Australian's Society Bride	Margaret Way
The Royal Marriage Arrangement	Rebecca Winters
Two Little Miracles	Caroline Anderson
Manhattan Boss, Diamond Proposal	Trish Wylie

HISTORICAL

Marrying the Mistress	Juliet Landon
To Deceive a Duke	Amanda McCabe
Knight of Grace	Sophia James

MEDICAL™

A Mummy for Christmas	Caroline Anderson
A Bride and Child Worth Waiting For	Marion Lennox
One Magical Christmas	Carol Marinelli
The GP's Meant-To-Be Bride	Jennifer Taylor
The Italian Surgeon's Christmas Miracle	Alison Roberts
Children's Doctor, Christmas Bride	Lucy Clark